"Stop!" The striden
around the bare hall
of Samantha's hand to cover her ears.

Samantha glanced back. It was him. The man who had broken into their room and then followed them into the store.

"Run!" Reid commanded, and her feet obeyed. "Get out."

She and Lily dashed past Reid. In her peripheral vision, she saw him turn and follow.

Lily grunted at Samantha's side, a step ahead.

At the door, she pushed it open and Lily ran through. As she jogged through, she turned to look back. The thug lumbered only two paces behind Reid.

Samantha moved aside as Reid stepped through the door. He swiveled around and grabbed the edge of the door, shoving it back toward the thug as he tried to step through. The heavy metal door collided with the thug's face with a resounding crack. He fell back and hit the floor. They watched for a moment, but the man didn't move.

By sixth grade, **Meghan Carver** knew she wanted to write. After a degree in English from Millikin University, she detoured to law school, completing a Juris Doctorate from Indiana University. She then worked in immigration law and taught college-level composition. Now, she homeschools her six children with her husband. When she isn't writing, homeschooling or planning another travel adventure, she is active in her church, sews and reads.

Books by Meghan Carver

Love Inspired Suspense

Under Duress

UNDER DURESS

MEGHAN CARVER

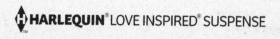

HARLEQUIN® LOVE INSPIRED® SUSPENSE

If you purchased this book without a cover you should be aware
that this book is stolen property. It was reported as "unsold and
destroyed" to the publisher, and neither the author nor the
publisher has received any payment for this "stripped book."

Recycling programs
for this product may
not exist in your area.

LOVE INSPIRED BOOKS

ISBN-13: 978-0-373-67736-8

Under Duress

Copyright © 2016 by Meghan Carver

All rights reserved. Except for use in any review, the reproduction
or utilization of this work in whole or in part in any form by any
electronic, mechanical or other means, now known or hereinafter
invented, including xerography, photocopying and recording, or in
any information storage or retrieval system, is forbidden without
the written permission of the editorial office, Love Inspired Books,
233 Broadway, New York, NY 10279 U.S.A.

This is a work of fiction. Names, characters, places and incidents are
either the product of the author's imagination or are used fictitiously, and
any resemblance to actual persons, living or dead, business establishments,
events or locales is entirely coincidental.

This edition published by arrangement with Love Inspired Books.

® and TM are trademarks of Love Inspired Books, used under license.
Trademarks indicated with ® are registered in the United States Patent
and Trademark Office, the Canadian Intellectual Property Office and in
other countries.

www.Harlequin.com

Printed in U.S.A.

Then they cried out to the Lord in their trouble,
And He saved them out of their distresses.
–Psalms 107:13

To Steve, my happily-ever-after.
You've been telling me to write a book for two decades.
Here you go. May there be many more.

To my children;
the Bigs for brainstorming and proofreading
and nagging me to "go write," and the Littles for their help
and obedience to the Bigs so I could "go write."

To my editor, Emily Rodmell.
Thank you for your encouragement, your wisdom
and your availability in The Search for a Killer Voice.
I'm honored that you saw potential in me.

To Love Inspired Historical author Angel Moore.
Thank you for believing I could write for
Love Inspired Suspense. Your encouragement and helpfulness
are invaluable. This story wouldn't exist without you.

To my writing friend and critique partner, Jenni Brummett.
Thank you for sharing with me the absolutely lovely way
you have with words. I appreciate the time and
energy you've funneled into this story and my life.

ONE

A scream tore through the humidity of the summer evening. Spikes of adrenaline pulsed through her veins as Samantha Callahan pressed hard on the accelerator of her little Honda to round the corner of the church building. She was late to pick up Lily, but the day camp director had agreed to look after Lily for the extra half hour.

The pickup area at the back of the church was empty save for a monster-size black SUV. On the sidewalk, a large man with a baseball cap pulled low and an open button-up shirt had his hands on her Lily. The tires on Samantha's car squealed in protest with the speed, and Lily looked up, her mouth open from her scream, relief washing across her features. The thug seemed to tighten his hold on the girl's skinny arm, jerking her closer to him. Red splotches radiated from beneath his grip.

Samantha stopped the Honda nose to nose

with the SUV and instinctively grabbed her bag. There wasn't time to consider her professional clothes wholly inappropriate for fighting bad guys, or her sensible but still high heels, which would make it difficult to run away. Lily pulled against the bully, but her thin frame barely allowed her to budge against his bulk.

Samantha swallowed, determined her voice would come out strong. "I don't know who you are, but she's not yours to take. Let her go."

The man stared at her, his eyes cut into narrow slits. Without looking away, he reached into his pocket and pulled out a photograph. He glanced down at the photograph then eyed her, his gaze sweeping from her hair to her shoes. Her skin crawled and itched as his attention swept over her.

Heat to match the summer afternoon rocketed up her back and neck. Whoever that man was, he wasn't only after Lily. He wanted her, too.

The curl of his lip projected pure maliciousness.

Her mind flitted to her phone, resting just inside the outside pocket of her large leather bag. There wasn't time to wait for an answer to a nine-one-one call. The thug would have them long gone by the time an emergency vehicle arrived.

She tossed a glance at Lily and nodded toward the car. The girl was smart. She would understand Samantha's meaning, that she should dive for the car as soon as she was loose.

The man took a step toward Samantha. She tightened her grip on the bag. "The girl is mine. I said let her go."

He took another step toward her, his hand still tight around Lily's arm. A breeze ruffled his shirt, and Samantha spied a weapon tucked in a shoulder holster. Moisture slicked her palms, and she choked up on the strap of her bag. How could she get this guy to let go and then get away without harm or injury?

Her bag. Of course. If he'd wanted to kill them, he could have easily accomplished that mission by now. All she needed was to get away.

"One last time." Her voice fairly growled. "Let her—let us—go."

One more step, and in a split second Samantha hefted her bag and swung wildly for the thug's head. He obviously didn't see it coming, for the metal buckle on the front of the tote ripped open his cheek, the contents of the bag clunking around inside. A shattering sound filled the void between them.

Bright red blood gushed down his cheek.

He let go of Lily, grabbing at his face with his hand. "You—"

Before he could finish, Samantha pulled Lily away from him. "Get in the car." She kept her voice low. "Now."

Her tennis shoes squeaking against the pavement, Lily jerked the closest back door open and dived headfirst into the backseat. With visual confirmation that Lily was crouching low, Samantha returned her attention to the thug just as he fixed his gaze back on her. She swung her bag again and hit him on the shoulder, praying that would buy her enough seconds to get in the car.

He seemed stunned that she would fight back, and she used those moments to rush to the driver's seat. With the door still flopping open, she threw the little Honda into Drive and slammed her foot against the accelerator. She scrunched down in the seat, staying just high enough to see over the steering wheel. "Stay down," she commanded Lily.

As she neared the curve that would lead her around the church building and to what she hoped and prayed was safety, the back windshield shattered. A bullet whizzed past the headrest and her ear.

A shriek filled the car. "Sam!"

"Lily? Are you hit?"

"No. You?"

"No." Samantha rounded the corner and rocketed through the front parking lot toward the road. A couple of loose pebbles smattered against the side panel. An engine roared behind her, and a glance in the rearview mirror revealed the SUV barreling toward her little car. The front parking lot was empty. There was no one to offer assistance. "Can you get up front and still stay low? Get my phone?" In her haste, she'd thrown her bag onto the front passenger seat. It had fallen onto the floor and was completely out of her reach.

Lily crawled in between the front seats. Samantha edged to the outside of her seat, allowing the girl as much maneuvering space as possible. Lily slid into the seat and crouched down, then retrieved the bag from the floor. She unzipped it and pulled out the phone, revealing a shattered screen. She turned it on and the screen glowed, but it didn't respond to her touch no matter how many times she tapped it.

"Can't call now." Lily dropped the phone back into the tote.

"At least it helped when I slugged that guy who grabbed you."

The normally busy highway had a small break in the traffic approaching, and Samantha hit the accelerator. She shot the little car in between a semi and a bread delivery truck. Lily grasped the armrest, leaning into Samantha with the force of the turn.

The black SUV screeched its tires and steered onto the shoulder next to the bread truck. When the truck swerved into oncoming traffic, the SUV slowed and eased out of view of Samantha's rearview mirror, probably behind the truck. Samantha gulped air. At least the SUV driver was smart enough to realize that an accident wouldn't benefit anybody.

But now what? It wouldn't be long before the SUV could catch up. What if that thug was crazy enough to drive alongside them and start shooting? Where was a policeman when she needed him? She would gladly pay a speeding ticket if a siren would just show up behind her. She catapulted another silent prayer, asking for help and safety and guidance.

Lily was still grasping the armrest, her breath ragged. "What now, Sam?"

"I'm thinking. Just hang on." Samantha released a hand from the wheel to swipe at the perspiration on her forehead. If she couldn't call a policeman, she would drive to one. In a tiny suburb like Heartwood Hill, the police station was only a couple of miles away, tucked in a corner of the city center and surrounded by grassy hills, playgrounds and picnic pavilions. She checked her mirrors again and allowed herself to lean back in the driver's seat when no monster SUV appeared. Maybe she had lost him.

She dared to point her attention at Lily for a moment. The girl seemed somewhat calm despite the turn of events. She was definitely a trouper, but then she had to be after the recent traumatic death of her father. It was in that church where Samantha had first met Lily and her father. She had been so drawn to the girl that she had stepped into her life as a mother figure. It had been an honor when Lily's father had asked if she would be Lily's guardian, if the need should ever arise. Now she recalled that he'd had an odd look about him, almost as if he'd expected that the need would be arising very soon. Samantha blinked hard and forced her attention back to the present. "So what happened back there?"

Lily drew a ragged breath. "I knew you'd be coming soon, so I decided to wait outside for you. Karen said it would be all right since she was just inside. I'd only been out there a few moments when that big truck pulled up and the guy got out. He offered me a lollipop to take a ride with him. You know, the kind with bubble gum inside?"

Samantha gripped the wheel and thanked

God that she had broached the don't-talk-to-strangers discussion with Lily just a few days after Lily had come to live with her. "That's your favorite."

"Yeah, but I'm not stupid. I'm ten years old now. I know better than to get in the car of someone I don't know."

"And?"

"And then he grabbed me, and you drove up."

Whoever the thug was, he wanted Lily. He even had a photo of her, possibly of them both. But why?

The winding drive that led back to the city buildings lay just up ahead. Gratitude filled Samantha's heart, thankfulness for safety around the corner and a soon-to-be daughter who listened to her. She wiped one hand on her leg and checked her mirrors again. No sign of—

"Watch out!" Lily's screech filled the car.

Samantha's chest cramped as she stomped on the brake. Her seat belt bit into the soft flesh of her neck, but it was too late. A burgundy Jeep Cherokee rose up in front of her. She fell back into the seat as the car's bumper smashed into the Jeep, a loud crumple heralding the collision.

She leaned her head against the window and swallowed, the lump in her throat crying out in protest. Who was driving the Jeep, and how could she and Lily get away now?

"Is this a problem, Sam?" Lily's voice sounded small in the sudden silence of the stillness.

"If the car won't drive anymore, yes. But maybe we can borrow his cell phone to call the police if we can't get going again." She threw the little car into Reverse and gently touched the gas, hoping to disengage her bumper from his and speed off to safety. Nothing. She surveyed the surrounding area, still a mile from the police station, but only homes dotted the edge of the grassy area, so far away that backyard barbecuers looked like ants milling around their patios. She paused, then reversed again, with a little more gas this time. Her Honda came loose with a loud grinding sound, but smoke began to trickle out from under the hood.

Once again, there was no one nearby that could be of help if needed.

No one except the guy she had just rear-ended.

Lily gawked with her face smooshed against the windshield and elbowed her. "He's ginormous." She paused, a frown wrinkling her forehead. "Is he safe?"

Samantha pushed her door open to see a

man of giant height unfold slowly from the Jeep as he removed his sunglasses. His face was clean shaven, although adorned with a scowl, and he was wearing a dark blue knit shirt with short sleeves that strained against his biceps. "I guess we'll find out." Despite his almost scary size, this had to be a far better encounter than their one with the guy who had a gun peeking out from under his shirt.

What other choice did she have? She would have to trust this man with the vaguely familiar face.

His first day back in town, and some crazy driver had to mangle his bumper? Reid Palmer shook his head and whispered a prayer for patience as his shoes hit the asphalt. The Lord certainly knew how practiced that request was, and Reid tamped down the niggling worry that he would never be free of making that particular supplication. Growing up with an abusive father hadn't helped him learn how to handle life with a calm and patient spirit. Anger had been his father's way of life, and Reid had thought it would be his, until he had met God. Then everything had changed, but prayer remained a constant companion.

A slight breeze, definitely not enough to dry the perspiration that beaded on his forehead, ruffled the strawberry blond hair of the woman stepping out of the compact car behind him. She frowned, but he couldn't tell if it was due to the impending storm or the damage to her car. Probably both. When their gazes collided, she narrowed her eyes at him. He wanted to step back or apologize at the force of her unspoken accusation, but he hadn't done anything wrong. She was the one who had rear-ended him.

He scrubbed a hand through his hair. Why did she look so familiar? It had been a few years since he'd been in Heartwood Hill, but he quickly ran through his mental contact list of faces from the area.

Law school. That was it. He'd attended a few classes with her and her twin. Which one she was he had no idea, but it didn't really matter. In the end, he would probably let her out of any responsibility for damage to his Jeep in the interest of forming amicable working relationships with the local lawyers, and they would part ways. In an hour, he'd be eating take-out Chinese and sitting on the floor of his new unfurnished apartment.

She leaned back into her car, talking to a girl in the front seat, probably retrieving her insurance card from the glove compartment and her phone to call local law enforcement. The girl clutched a large leather bag and shared a worried look with the redhead. Reid shot up another prayer, this time that the woman wouldn't call the police to write up an accident report. There was no need to involve law enforcement, and one encounter with a person from his past was enough for this evening. He didn't want to face that difficult reintroduction sooner than he had planned.

The redhead straightened and hurried toward him, but her attention focused everywhere but on him. She glanced over her shoulder twice as she walked the short distance. Reid's training whispered to him that she had the manner of a person afraid someone was after her. He peered past her, but nothing suspicious presented itself.

Without a greeting, she asked, "Can I borrow your phone? Mine got damaged, and I need to call the police."

He reached toward his pocket for the cell. "I think you need a tow truck more than—"

A scream of tires interrupted him. The redhead gasped and spun around. A moment later, she signaled to the girl in her passenger seat. The girl slid out of the car and rounded the front in a jog, a purple backpack clutched to her front. When the girl was within reach, the redhead nudged her toward Reid's Jeep.

Whatever was going on, this woman was scared to a degree Reid hadn't seen in a long time. He leaned around her and spied a large black SUV completing a turn, its driver gunning the engine. There were no outward indicators that the SUV was after them, but the woman and girl scrambling into his backseat were an obvious clue that something was wrong.

With her hand on the door handle, the woman whispered to him, "Get us out of here. Now." She glanced back again, a hunted look creasing the area around her eyes. "Please."

Was this for real? This woman rear-ends his Jeep and then jumps into his backseat and demands he drive her away from whoever is pursuing her? It was like an action movie where the hunky hero saves the girl and they drive off into the sunset together. Except he was no hunk or hero, and he could guarantee that they wouldn't drive off into a happily-ever-after together.

He stared at her, immobile, as she pushed the girl into his backseat and then clambered in behind her. She slammed the door shut, then rolled down the tinted window a couple of inches. She poked her lips up to the opening to growl at him. "Come on!"

Apparently he was moving too slowly for

her liking. He cut-timed to the driver's door and slid into the seat. The engine roared to life, and as he pulled away, the bumper of the woman's compact car dropped to the ground with a clamoring clunk.

From her hunched position in the back, the redhead held on to the shoulder of his seat. "I'm so sorry to impose. I don't normally jump into other people's vehicles and bark at them to drive. But we're being chased by that black SUV, and we had to get away." She threaded her free arm around the girl's shoulders. "I will not let them take my Lily."

In the rearview mirror, Reid saw Lily lean into the woman. He stifled the urge to wrinkle his nose. In the enclosed vehicle with the air-conditioning blowing, an odor wafted from Lily as if she had been camping and hadn't showered for a few days.

The redhead turned to peer out the back window, drawing Reid's gaze back to her car, abandoned in the turn lane of the busy road. The black SUV had pulled off in front of it, and a man with a blue ball cap was stalking the perimeter of the car, peering into the windows.

"That's him. He chased us all the way from the church." She twisted back to the front, seeming to realize where they were. "We need to get to the police station. It'll be safe there."

Reid gripped the wheel, an unsettling sensation seizing his middle. "Have you called nine-one-one?"

"No. I smashed my phone when I hit that guy with my purse to get him to let go of Lily." She swiped her hand across her lips. "Can we call the police with your phone?"

"Sure." Reid startled at how quickly he'd answered. After his multiple motorcycle crashes and resignation from the local police force a few years back, he wasn't eager to make contact with local law enforcement, but the woman needed help. He commanded his hands to relax on the steering wheel and his voice to take a gentle tone. "In a minute. Let's just talk about this first and see if we can figure out what's happened." Reid signaled to turn left, watching to see that the SUV wasn't following. Now would be the proper time for introductions, a time to reassure her that she could trust him. But she hadn't recognized his name earlier, and he wasn't ready yet to remind her of his identity. "Why don't you tell me why you're in my backseat?"

"There's not much to tell. I was picking Lily up from a day camp at church, and the guy in that big SUV had his hands on her when I pulled up. I jumped out of my car to stop him and ended up hitting him in the face with my bag." She hefted the leather tote to show him. "I think the buckle hit him because there was blood on his face. That gave us time to get away, but he shot out the back window of my car. I thought we had lost him in the traffic on the way to the police station, but then I hit you, and here we are." She paused to take a deep breath. "I have no idea who he is or why he would want us."

Kidnapping. Pure and simple. If the man had wanted them dead, he could have done it right there in the parking lot. But the motive was a mystery. Why them, and what did he want?

"You're safe now."

"Thanks for letting us jump in your car. By the way, I'm Samantha Callahan, and this is Lily, my soon-to-be daughter. I'm her guardian right now, but I have the adoption in the works."

Of course, Samantha. One of the Callahan twins and the smartest in their law class. He should have known by her assertiveness that she wasn't the sweet and optimistic Mallory.

She scanned the passing buildings as they merged into a commercial area. "You've passed the police station. If you turn right up here, we can circle around."

Reid sucked in a breath. There was no avoiding it. "You don't need the police."

"Why not?" Her hand clutched the back of his seat, pulling the fabric away from his shoulder. "You look familiar. Who are you?"

He turned as Lily leaned against the back of the front seat. "Are you a giant? You're really big. I don't think I know anyone as big as you."

That was a new one. But then he hadn't spent much time around kids who spoke their minds freely. Maybe this was a perfectly acceptable question.

Samantha shushed her. "You can't go around asking a stranger if he's a giant. Maybe we need to work on your manners."

"What's wrong with that? I'm making conversation. I'm trying to look him in the eye, but he's driving. And I didn't get a chance to try out my firm handshake since you shoved me in the car. I'm being polite."

"Lily." She dragged out the last syllable.

Reid held up a hand. "It's fine." He turned enough to meet Lily's gaze for a nanosecond then returned his attention to the road. In his peripheral vision, he caught her smile. "No, I'm not a giant, technically. I'm only six feet four inches tall."

He met Samantha's gaze in the rearview mirror and forced a lopsided grin. Frustration glinted in her blue eyes. "I'm Reid Palmer," he repeated. "We attended our first year at law school together."

The color slid from her face, and she licked her lips before she could recover her composure. "Reid." She drew out his name as if fighting to keep her tone steady. "Yes."

She sat back against the seat and turned her attention to the window.

His mind blanked on what to say as he surveyed the surrounding area for the big SUV. A simple you-can-trust-me speech seemed inadequate. They hadn't known each other well in school, but from what she probably remembered of him, her anxiety was warranted. Mere words wouldn't matter to her now.

Samantha swiped a hand through her hair. "I still need to involve the authorities. At least file a report or something."

It wasn't exactly the timing he had hoped for to make amends with his buddies. But he couldn't just drop her off. And even though he hadn't witnessed what had happened at the church, he'd seen the black SUV that was after them.

Another thought niggled the back of his mind. This was his chance to prove to himself that he had changed since the last time he was in town. That his personal dragons had been slayed. That even though he didn't trust himself in a romantic relationship, he was a gentleman not only capable of protecting and serving but also eager to do so.

For her own safety, he had to convince her that she could trust him. This wasn't exactly the way he wanted to be reunited with his former brothers on the force, but it was too late to enact his original plan of bringing gifts of a case of pop and a couple buckets of chicken wings. Dark thunder-boomers dotted the sky, scudding and bumping into one large mass, as Reid turned his Jeep toward the police station. The first streak of lightning jagged across the sky.

TWO

"If you aren't taking us to the police as I requested, then legally, we're still kidnapped." Samantha's tone of accusation cut to his core, and Reid swiped his hand across his jeans to keep from digging his fingernails into the flesh of his palm.

He surveyed the side and rearview mirrors, but they appeared to be free from a tail. The storm clouds gathering out the front windshield mirrored the foreboding in his soul. There was a storm coming, and it wasn't going to be just a gentle rain.

A growl threatened to escape from his throat, but he tamped it down. He shouldn't be surprised at her accusation. Lawyers excelled at pointing the finger and sidestepping the blame. But neither could he let her place sole fault on him. "Fine." He pointed out the windshield. "Notice we're headed toward the station. But remember, you're the one who jumped into my backseat. What was I supposed to do? Kick you out?"

"You were supposed to take us straight to safety. To the police station." She enunciated her words carefully, as if giving instructions to a three-year-old. "And it was either you or that thug."

"From what you tell me, there's nothing for the police to go on. You don't have any identifying characteristics. You don't know the model of his black SUV. You don't have a license plate number. Chances are excellent, if he didn't peel out and leave tire marks in the parking lot, that he left no evidence at the church. And it sounds as though a bullet didn't lodge anywhere in your car." She was definitely in a predicament. A sense of foreboding settled between his shoulder blades as he turned toward the station.

"Wait." Hope tinged her voice as she reached toward the girl. "We could tell you what he was wearing, a button-up shirt that hung open enough to reveal his holster. And a blue baseball cap with a white horseshoe on the front."

"Yeah, he was kinda mean looking." Lily pushed hair off her forehead. "I'm sure I'd recognize him again."

"Of course you would, sweetie."

Reid grimaced. They were probably fist-bumping in his backseat, feeling victorious regarding their evidence. Now was definitely not the time to mention the unreliability of eyewitness accounts.

Reid turned his head to look out his side window before he rolled his eyes. No need to rile Samantha up any more than she was already. "You mean an Indianapolis Colts hat?"

"That's it."

"That's no good." He approached the intersection where Samantha had rear-ended his Jeep moments ago. The SUV was gone, and he turned onto the road that led to the police station. "At least half the men in the greater Indianapolis area own that hat." He turned and nodded toward the back. "Reach under the passenger seat."

Samantha disappeared from his rearview mirror as she leaned toward the floor. A loud exhalation later, her hand appeared over the seat, grasping a blue baseball cap with a white horseshoe on the front.

"There has to be something to go on. Evidence at the crime scene, or maybe I could work with a sketch artist?"

"Was he wearing sunglasses? Did he have a mustache or beard that he could shave off?" She'd been watching too many police procedurals on TV. A cop's life wasn't that exciting. It included long stretches of boredom and paperwork followed by a lapse in judgment caused by too much anger and then a career change. Case closed. He corked the sigh that threatened to bubble up.

"Well, at least we're headed in the right direction. The police will help us."

"Sam, I'm starving. Can we stop to eat?" The quiet voice piped up from the backseat.

"How can we stop to eat when we don't know where the bad guy is, Lily? We have to get safe first. Talk to the police. Then we eat."

Reid hadn't been around children much, but when he had been about that size, his appetite had been insatiable. He patted his stomach and noted that the time on the dashboard clock did indicate it was past suppertime.

He pulled the Jeep up to the front of the redbrick station and parked in the empty lot. "Don't get out yet. Let me check around." He surveyed the area in his mirrors, then turned and stared out the back windshield for several minutes. Dread twisted in his abdomen, but Samantha was right. She ought to at least make initial contact with the police. If she needed them later, it would be helpful that they already knew her name.

A couple of police motorcycles were parked just inside a tall gate to the side of the building. Disturbing memories riddled his brain like so many bullets. Three separate times he had disregarded police policy that condemned a reckless disregard for safety and taken a motorcycle over one hundred miles per hour. Far over that limit, in fact. The last time, he hadn't even caught the suspect, and in his anger at his failure had raged against the bike, pushing it to the ground and kicking it, until he'd severely damaged it. His chief had not looked kindly on the destruction of property and suggested he resign his position. Reid shook his head as if that could dislodge the images.

"It looks clear. I doubt a suspected perp like that would get too close to the station anyway. Let's go."

The three slid out of the vehicle, and Samantha held Lily's hand as they approached the front door.

Inside, a lone officer in uniform sat behind a tall countertop. The Friday-night shift at the front desk was usually a lonely one. The officer pushed aside his hunting magazine and first looked over Samantha and then slanted his eyes at Reid. "Well, well, well. Back in town?"

"Cody." Reid gave him a polite nod. "How you been?"

"Better'n you, I suspect. Still got my shield

and weapon." He tapped two fingers on the badge fixed on his uniform. "Heard you got religion."

Samantha slid him a funny look as if she wasn't too sure of the direction of the conversation or what it had to do with her predicament. She probably doubted the religion part as well, considering what she'd known of him in law school.

Reid felt the muscle tic in his jaw but forced a polite tone. "You could say that." In his peripheral vision, he saw Samantha's eyes widen. That was enough catching up, though, for the visit had nothing to do with him. It was about getting help for Samantha and Lily.

It wouldn't go over well with Cody if the old Reid reared his ugly head and reached across the counter to punch some sense into him. The new Reid shoved his hands into his pants pockets and focused on the need next to him, the red-haired beauty in the summer skirt with flowers all over it. "As glad as I am to be back in Heartwood Hill, this isn't really about me. My friend and her daughter need your assistance. Why don't I just wait over here in case they need me, and you can help them?" He took a step back.

This wasn't the way he had wanted it to go. He had planned to call an old buddy he thought might receive him better, someone who would be willing to ease him back into communication. He watched Samantha step up to the counter, her arm curled around Lily's thin shoulders. Samantha deserved better than this. She shouldn't have to suffer because of his past impropriety as an officer with the Heartwood Hill Police Department. Cody always was a bit high-and-mighty, but Reid couldn't change who was pulling desk duty that night. A fresh wave of regret and repentance sloshed through him. Now Samantha had to pay for his past mistakes and poor choices.

He took another step back to distance his past from the present.

Why would Reid be treated like this at the police station? What had he done to deserve being snubbed?

Samantha had thought that the police were always supposed to be helpful and friendly. The bright white walls, fluorescent lights and tall, clean counter of the reception area certainly spoke of professionalism. A tall potted plant by a window added a touch of hospitality. But officers were people, too, with their own troubles and dramas happening in their worlds. Perhaps this Cody had had a bad day, had been chewed out by his superior or was suffering the effects of a fight with his girl-friend. Whatever the history between the two, Reid at least deserved some common courtesy.

Of one thing she was relatively sure: the thug who had tried to kidnap them wouldn't dare to enter the police station to get her.

But considering this officer's dubious attitude, she had a sudden surge of gratitude for Reid's calm handling of the accident and his acceptance of her jump into his backseat. That, and his ability to defend her if needed, judging by his muscular physique.

Cody leaned toward her on the desk with a pointed look at her empty ring finger. "So, miss, maybe now that we've got that guy out of the way, why don't you tell me your name?"

Samantha took a deep breath. Now she was getting somewhere. "Samantha Callahan, and this is Lily—"

"And is there a Mr. Callahan?"

"My father, but what does that have to do with—"

"Are you injured?" His penetrating gaze crawled over her hair and face. "'Cause you look as if you're in pretty good shape to me." A crazy grin tilted across his face.

"I'm fine. No injuries." Why wasn't he getting out the proper forms? A large file storage unit hung on the wall at the end of the counter, filled with neat stacks of preprinted papers. "But shouldn't something be done? That's why I asked Mr. Palmer to drive me here."

Cody held up his hands in a surrender gesture. "Fine. Yes. Tell me what happened."

She repeated her story, including the Colts baseball cap and how she'd jumped in the back of Reid's Jeep Cherokee. She finished with a plea. "Please, Officer, I don't know if that guy is still out there. He might be waiting for us. What happens next?"

He flipped through some forms in the wall unit and selected one, then retrieved a pen from a cup on the counter and pushed both toward Samantha. "Fill out your name, address, phone number and email. Then write down here—" he jabbed at the bottom half of the paper "—what you remember about the incident. Include what happened, in detail, and who might have seen it."

Samantha glanced back at Reid. He leaned against the wall next to the door and shrugged at her, but a telltale crease in his brow conveyed his concern for her treatment here. She turned back to the officer. She risked making the situation with Cody worse, but she had to ask. "Is there anyone else I can talk to?"

"You don't need anyone else, 'cause they'll all say the same. Fill out the form." He tossed a smirk at Reid then returned his focus to Samantha. "But if you want to come back when my shift ends at eleven, I'd be happy to help you personally with whatever you need."

She just couldn't stop it. She rolled her eyes, so far back and at such a speed that pain shot through her skull. There was some big guy out there trying to kidnap her and Lily, and now she had to deal with a reunion with Reid Palmer, a man who would never have been voted Most Likely to Succeed in law school. The last thing she needed in her life right now was some tough guy trying to pick her up. Between her father's betrayal and her—ahem—near indiscretion in college, she had had enough of bad boys thinking they were tough and desirable and strutting around like peacocks.

Fine. She plastered on a smile as she completed the form. No sense in burning bridges, although she wasn't sure any bridge had even been built. "I can't leave a phone number because my screen is shattered and the phone won't receive any calls."

A throat cleared behind her, and Reid stepped up to the counter. "Put down my phone number." He scribbled on the form and passed it to Cody. "I'll make sure she gets any information if you call me."

Cody hesitated but reached into a drawer and withdrew a business card. He handed it to Samantha. "You can call this number to check for updates, but if you find yourself in an emergency, of course call nine-one-one." He skimmed the paper. "We'll send an officer to the church, but there isn't much we can do at this point."

"Thank you for your help." She turned away from the desk and toward the door, pulling on Lily's hand. She stared at the rectangular shape, a portal into a world that was now dark with storm clouds and filled with foreboding. Where would she and Lily be sleeping tonight if that thug found them? Would they be sleeping at all? Nothing had changed, though, in his intentions. He had had the chance to kill them, and he hadn't. If the bad guy was smart at all, he would know where they lived. And once he got whatever he was after, then what would he do?

Reid pushed away from the wall and opened the door, a look of disappointment etched across his face. At least he wasn't saying, "I told you so."

Cody's last jeer propelled her toward the exit. "Let your boyfriend take you home."

Boyfriend?

She pushed outside, Lily in tow. Reid's voice

filtered over the couple of cars driving past on the street as he said a cordial "see you later" to the officer. She stopped abruptly on the bottom step and scanned the parking lot. Lily rested her head against Samantha's arm. The poor girl was probably tired, hungry and scared. Samantha would have to be strong for her. Tears threatened, stinging the backs of her eyelids. The only thing she could do now was call a cab and go home. The problems with that plan were that she had no phone to call with, and Heartwood Hill didn't have a cab service. The suburb was so small there wasn't even a bus system. She could call a cab from Indianapolis, but how long would she have to wait, and how much would she have to pay? She refused to wait inside the police station with Cody.

She jabbed a tear from her cheek. She probably shouldn't go home, though. Surely that man with the gun would find her eventually.

A gentle hand touched her shoulder. Reid stepped in front of her. "Can I give you a ride?"

An answer stalled in her throat. If she accepted his offer of a ride, she didn't need a phone or a cab. Problem solved. Then why was she having trouble answering? She swiped a hair off her cheek as the truth stabbed at her heart. She worked too much, bringing forever families together through adoption. As wonderful as that was, it didn't allow for much of a social life or the formation of friendships with girlfriends she could call for help at a moment's notice. She was estranged from her father. Hadn't spoken to him in more than a year. And her most reliable relationships, with her mother and her twin sister, wouldn't help her now since they were on the other side of the country at a church conference.

For a reason she couldn't fathom, she didn't want to share that information with Reid.

She wanted to tell him that she didn't need the help of any man. That her father's betrayal and desertion when she was just a teenager had torn a hole in her heart. That the guy in college who had turned out to be such a manipulator had ripped that gap wide-open.

She must have been scowling because a confused, even sad, expression shadowed Reid's face. Was he hurt by her silence? She had been treated so callously over the years that there was no way she would bring her wall down now.

But neither did she want to be rude. She took a deep breath and forced herself to look into Reid's vivid blue eyes. "I would appreciate that." His strong presence was comforting, even though she didn't want to admit it.

She slid into the front seat of the Jeep as

Lily climbed into the back. This time it was a bit more willingly, but then why were her palms slicked with perspiration? As her seat belt clicked into place, she shot up a prayer that Reid would be more helpful than the officer at the station.

And that he'd left his bad-boy persona in his past.

THREE

Reid scrubbed a hand over his face and down his neck. Since they had left the station a scant ten minutes ago, that girl, Lily, had talked of half a dozen things including her favorite book, her new shoes and how hard it was to remember the multiplication tables. He should probably be grateful that she felt safe and comfortable in his ride. Perhaps those feelings would transfer over to her guardian, who even now refused to relax against the back of the seat and kept darting her gaze to the left and to the right.

The low-fuel bell dinged. Reid slumped his shoulders. Now? He turned toward his passengers but kept his view on the road. "We have to get gas first, and then we'll figure this out. But you should be thinking of who you can stay with tonight."

"Stay with?" Samantha sounded doubtful of anything other than going home.

"Like a sleepover? The late, late movie with popcorn and snacks." Lily wiggled in her seat.

"We'll see." But Samantha sounded just like his own mother when she really meant "no way."

Reid meticulously obeyed the speed limit for a couple of miles from the station, out toward the interstate and a long array of commercial offerings. He pulled into the least expensive gas station and hit the brake next to the pump on the end, closest to the exit. His original plan had been to drive straight to his new digs and eat something cheap, like chow mein. His cash had to last him until he could secure a family law client base or an actual position, and he certainly hadn't planned on chauffeuring an old school acquaintance around this evening, not even one with strawberry blond hair and an adorable smattering of freckles across her nose.

Before he put the Jeep into Park, he surveyed the street and surrounding businesses. Samantha was right to be cautious, but there was no sign of a large black SUV. In fact, there weren't any black vehicles at all. He cut the engine and left the keys in the ignition. "I'd rather not have to get gas right now, but better this than being stranded on the side of the road. You two stay in the Jeep. Leave the windows up and stay low."

Before he had the door half-open, the girl whined again from the backseat. "I'm hungry, Sam. Can't I run inside and get a bag of chips and a pop? Maybe some of those little chocolate cupcakes or a candy bar? You know, something to tide me over until we get wherever we're going." Her voice took on a wheedling tenor. "I can get something for you, too."

Reid shook his head. What a study in the art of cajoling. He turned to see Samantha shaking her head no and reaching through the front seats to pat Lily's hand. "We'll get something soon, I promise. But Mr. Palmer is right. We don't want to take any chances. We don't know that we're out of danger."

Irritation at the predicament of an innocent woman and her ward bubbled up from a place deep within that he kept buried. A burial ground that concealed a childhood at the hands of an angry father, the very reason he had pursued a career in law enforcement so many years ago. There was no way he would allow himself to call that emotion what it truly was, even if he was fighting the urge to slam his fist into the dashboard. And what about that salvation that had swept over him just in time to save him from the dire consequences of himself? A verse bubbled up as he prayed, again, for peace and calm. *The effective, fervent prayer of a righteous man avails much.*

He glanced around the pumps one more time and slammed his door shut. What was this ride, though, if it wasn't a favor? A rescue, even? Samantha probably thought he deserved that callous treatment. People with flawless pasts and perfect lives often looked down their noses at those who had had to fight for every inch of progress. And so far as he could tell, Samantha Callahan had lived a perfect life.

A few long strides carried him across the stretch of gas station asphalt as he pinched the front of his shirt to fan away the summer heat. Inside the convenience store, he prepaid twenty bucks. It would have to do for now, at least until he figured out what to do with his ride-along.

Samantha hissed out a sigh and turned in her seat, peeking around the headrest but making sure she was hidden behind it. Reid was gone for a few moments, and then he strode back to the pump without even a glance in her direction. A scowl resided on his face. He was probably grouchy, irritated to have the two of them in his vehicle without a place to go. Whatever his plans had been, they hadn't included Samantha and Lily.

She picked at a fingernail. She probably had come across to him as just as grouchy. She usually did to people who knew her twin. Mallory, the forever optimist, the sweet, sunshine-and-daisies twin. It didn't matter how friendly she tried to be, Samantha was the one who everyone perceived as serious and stoic. Add on to that a past filled with men who acted like jerks, and, well, it was enough to make a girl want to leave town and start over, except that she loved her twin as much as everyone else.

Numbers ticked by on the gas pump, and Samantha scanned the station again. Reid had taken them to the police, and it had turned out exactly like he had said. The police, or at least that one officer, had thought there wasn't much they could do.

She dug back into the recesses of her mind, trying to dredge up memories of Reid. Even by law school, she had decided she didn't need any men in her life, so she had largely ignored those around her, choosing instead to focus on her studies and her sister and mother. Reid was a bit older than she was and had had a different career before entering law school. But that wasn't unusual, and she couldn't remember anything else. Whatever his history, his reason for leaving the school had been the year's scandal.

"Sam?"

Lily's quiet voice broke through her reverie. "Hmm?"

"Do you know Mr. Palmer?"

Samantha craned her arm around the side of the seat to rub Lily's back in what she hoped was a comforting gesture. However much Samantha needed reassurance that all would be well, Lily needed it more. "Sort of. We went to law school together for a year, but that was a while ago."

"Can we trust him?"

Smart kid. "For now, I guess. He's at least better than the guy who tried to nab you at the church. And he's been more helpful than the officer at the station."

Lily pointed toward the busy street. "Why don't we just get out and run to one of the fast-food places over there? Get away from Mr. Palmer and the bad guy, call someone for a ride, go home?"

"That's an interesting plan, but we don't want to bother any friends. We've already bothered Mr. Palmer, and that's quite enough." It wasn't something she wanted to admit often, but her dedication to her work came before friends. There was too much good to be done in the field of family law, helping desperate would-be parents secure forever families and uniting abandoned children with loving mothers and fathers, that she couldn't justify taking personal time to cultivate relationships. In fact, Samantha couldn't name anybody she could bother with a situation of this magnitude, especially with her immediate family on a trip so far away. "I want you to scrunch down back there. Don't let your head pop up from behind the seat."

Lily slouched down, and Samantha raised the headrest a couple of inches so she could stay low behind it and still perform her surveillance. She wasn't sure why, but she thought it was best to monitor what happened behind the vehicle rather than the front, even though Reid was in that direction at the gas pump. Surely it had nothing to do with his thick black hair and the navy polo that hugged his torso. Nothing at all to do with the protectiveness and feeling of security that emanated from him. Definitely nothing to do with his clean, soapy scent that lingered in the Jeep.

She shook her attention away from Reid just as a monster black SUV pulled into a spot two pumps away.

"Get down. More," she whispered to Lily.

Samantha clutched the seat fabric with shaking hands as she jerked down behind the seat. Was that the same SUV from the church? Reid was still out there. Would the thug recognize him from the accident site? His Jeep?

She licked some moisture to her lips and inched up until she could see Reid through the space between the seat and the headrest. How could she just hide there and do nothing when Reid might give them away? Was he safe out there? The windows weren't tinted enough to assure her that she and Lily were hidden, because she could still read the numbers on the pump ticking by and see Reid leaning against the Jeep, his face to the pump.

A burly man stepped out of the SUV. He had removed his Colts cap and now wore wrap-around sunglasses, but he was definitely the guy from the church parking lot and the site of the accident. The only reason a guy would wear sunglasses with thunderstorm clouds colliding overhead and nighttime settling over the town would be to avoid detection. If only her phone still worked, she could snap a picture, an image for Cody to run through facial recognition or something high-tech like that.

A screech squeaked out, and Samantha clapped her hand over her own mouth.

A second man wearing similar sunglasses emerged from the passenger side of the SUV and jogged inside the station, Samantha assumed to pay in advance with cash. She sagged in the seat. There were two guys after them now? The one hadn't got them, so he'd brought in reinforcements? A few seconds later, he tossed a thumbs-up at the first thug. He lifted the nozzle and turned toward his vehicle, pausing, nozzle in hand, as he seemed to notice Reid. Samantha couldn't track his eye movements with such heavy sunglasses and the tint of the Jeep's windows, but his head turned a little as if he were studying the Jeep. Then his attention appeared to return to Reid.

Her throat constricted and, gasping for air, Samantha slid over to the driver's seat, working her skirt over the gearshift with trembling fingers. Staying low, she leaned toward the crack in the driver's-side door and called to Reid in a stage whisper. "Reid! He's here. That guy from the church. Are you done? I'm in the driver's seat now."

Samantha tilted her head to peer through the sliver of open door. Reid seemed to stay calm as he surveyed the gas station. Keeping it low, he held a hand out, palm facing her, as if to say that he'd heard her and she should stay quiet.

She twisted to dare another look at the thugs—plural now. The first, looking at the second, nodded in their direction. The first replaced the nozzle in the pump as if trying to act normal, then began a slow advance toward Reid.

The second man slammed his passenger-side door shut a moment later, the thud reverberating through the Jeep like the thunder that threatened in the clouds, and headed their way.

Reid jerked the Jeep's backseat door open and jumped in. "Go!"

Samantha jumped at the rough sound of his command and sat upright. Her pulse quickened in her veins. "What about the nozzle?"

"Trust me. Go!"

She bit her lip, threw the Jeep into Drive and mashed the accelerator. The vehicle lunged forward. The nozzle broke free from the gas tank and clanked against the pump. At the sound, she hit the brakes.

The squeal of the tires on the pavement made her want to clutch at her ears.

"Go!" Another command from Reid, more terse this time. A glance in the rearview mirror revealed his position of surveillance. Lily crouched down in her corner of the backseat. "They know we're here. They're back in their SUV and following us." Reid swiveled around and pointed out to the busy road. "Get out there. In the middle of traffic."

Samantha pulled away from the pump and

nosed onto the highway, the black SUV filling the rearview mirror. Reid wanted her to get into the middle of traffic? Fine. But she prayed that the Lord would steer for her because she didn't trust her shaking hands to maintain a grip.

She urged the Jeep across two lanes of oncoming traffic, narrowly missing a minivan. She jerked the wheel to turn into the fast lane, and the Jeep teetered as if two wheels had left the ground.

A UPS truck shot up next to her in the right lane. Where had that come from? The steering wheel fought against her as she struggled to right the Jeep, but her slick palms slipped off the wheel.

The brown side panel of the truck filled the windshield and passenger-side window. She slammed the brakes. The Jeep screeched in a collision course with the truck.

"Lily!" It was her last utterance before she closed her eyes and braced for impact.

FOUR

That woman was going to get them all killed.

From the backseat, Reid pushed his chest against the side of the driver's seat, shoved his cheek against the side of the headrest and stretched his arms around Samantha to grab the wheel. Yet another instance where his six-foot-four-inch height gave him an edge, not to mention the quick reflexes from the police training he had tried to leave behind. The UPS truck swerved away from the Jeep as Reid jerked the steering wheel hard to the left, almost willing the Jeep's four tires back onto the ground out of sheer desperation.

No way was he going to die here and now. Not Samantha and Lily, either, if he had anything to do with it.

He righted the Jeep into the proper position in the left lane, his attention pulled to the rearview mirror with a screech of tires behind them. The black SUV had catapulted into traffic, as well. It was now only one car behind them.

Reid forced his focus to the road before them and calmed his breathing to short puffs. Samantha's hair fluffed in and out with his huffs, the scent of cleanliness and sunshine that emanated from it distracting him in a way he wasn't familiar with. Apparently, he'd lost some of his edge.

"Thanks." Samantha's voice wobbled. "I thought that was going to be the end of us."

Reid swerved into the right lane. He would signal if he could reach it, but Samantha didn't seem to be in any condition to follow orders. "He's still behind us. We're not done yet." At the very least, she needed to be able to concentrate enough to manage the speed of the vehicle.

"We're alive." She relaxed her head against his straining biceps, probably seeking rest and comfort. But immediately she jerked upright as if realizing the intimacy, and the inappropriate timing, of the gesture. Her foot must have pressed the accelerator because the Jeep rushed forward.

"Slow! Don't rear-end that car."

Samantha let up and the Jeep eased up on the compact car it had almost trampled. "Sorry."

"We're alive, but not safe yet. Pray." He

squeezed his eyes shut for a split second and then refocused on the road. No way could he let himself get distracted now, not with a maniacal thug following them on a busy street and his life still resting in Samantha's ability to accelerate and brake at the right times. It was Friday night in a small town and apparently everyone had decided to eat out and hit the movie theater tonight.

Hide. That was a temporary solution. Where could they pull off and sit to avoid detection and to figure out what to do next? A row of semis stretched ahead of him. He pointed without lifting his hand from the wheel. "Slower. Get in between the trucks."

Samantha gently touched the brake, and he cut back to the left lane, now two vehicles in front of the SUV. One of them was a jacked-up monster truck. The thing was so tall it completely hid the black SUV from view. It was perfect.

"I think I can take over the steering again now." Samantha gripped the wheel below his fists as if the force of her hands would convince Reid.

Lily scooted forward in her seat. "But he has his arms around you, Sam. His really long and muscular arms. Ooo—"

"Lily, that's enough." She turned her head to

glare at the girl, her freckles dark and prominent in the stormy early-evening gloom, her face inches from Reid's. A pink blush touched her cheeks, and she faced forward again. "I'll be fine, Reid."

"All right. Let's pass these two semis—"

Lightning flashed to the ground nearby as a shock wave of thunder ripped through the low-hanging clouds. Samantha startled and landed their front tire in the lane of oncoming traffic. Reid jumped for the steering wheel again and swerved them back to safety. "You're fine?" Try as he might, he couldn't keep the critical tone from his voice.

"It surprised me. I was going to get us back in our lane." She puffed her hair away from her face. "I'm not just a helpless female."

"Slow down some more. We're going to turn right soon." That was the second time she had just about gotten them all killed, but even his limited knowledge of women dictated that he shouldn't voice that thought.

Two semis up, he jagged back to the right lane, squeezing in between two of the long trucks. "Take it easy. Get ready for a turn." Samantha pushed the brake, and a split second later, he steered right toward a fast-food restaurant.

He nodded toward a parking spot. "We're

headed in there. Hit the brake again." He eased into the opening behind a large cargo van with All Righty Plumbing painted on the side. Samantha hit the brake just as the front tires bumped against the curb.

Sure now of Samantha's hands on the wheel and her foot on the brake, he released his grip and spun to the back window. The black SUV was still trailing the last semi, caught behind a minivan driven by an elderly woman who couldn't see over the steering wheel, tooling along below the speed limit. Without even a glance into the parking lot, the thug drove past them.

Reid turned back to the front and collapsed against the backseat, flexing his fingers to loosen the soreness out after his death grip on the steering wheel.

Lily popped up over the back of the seat and eyed the restaurant. "Are we safe? Does this mean we're going to eat now?"

Samantha shifted into Park and leaned her head against the rest. "Let us catch our breath first, girl."

"And give the bad guy a few minutes to get farther away." He had the strange but undeniable urge to ruffle her hair, but would a ten-year-old girl see that as affectionate? As relief that they were all safe? Or was she at the age where her hairstyle was of the utmost importance and all touching would be an affront? Considering that she had the pungent aroma of someone who had been running and playing and fishing all day, he doubted it was the latter.

But what was he thinking anyway? She wasn't his. He had just met her maybe an hour ago, and under rather unusual circumstances. And even though he knew her guardian a little, Samantha probably didn't have a favorable memory of him.

Samantha ran her hand through her hair and fluffed out the ends. Reid noticed again the clean scent of shampoo that emanated from her. It was the best scent he'd had in his Jeep... well, ever. He breathed deeply, desperate to inhale peace and calm. Samantha was a smart attorney, well practiced at asking tough questions.

He was a smart attorney, too. He knew what was coming.

It was unavoidable.

Samantha turned in the driver's seat, pulling her knee up toward the console. She pierced Reid with a classic interrogation look. "So you want to tell me what was going on back there at the police station?"

He shrugged, trying to appear nonchalant

even as his stomach roiled. "I tried to tell you that they wouldn't be helpful. But I apologize for any difficulty my presence caused. I figured it might…uh…stifle their desire to serve and protect."

Samantha cocked her head, her brow furrowed. "Why?"

"I was a police officer." He paused. Held his breath. "I was asked to leave the force."

Of course. Samantha remembered now. That had been his job before law school. He was a police officer. And now his hesitancy to drive them to the police station as well as his knowledge of evidence became clear, as well. Samantha sagged against her seat. She had forced him into an uncomfortable, even awkward, situation for which he was unprepared because she hadn't trusted his judgment.

"The force?" Lily leaned against the seat.

"Lily, he means the police force. The police department." Samantha swiped some hair from her cheek.

"You were a police officer?" Apparently, her charge wasn't going to let go of this easily. "Did you carry a gun?" Lily strained forward in her curiosity. "Do you have a gun now?"

Reid cleared his throat. "Since we're all getting hungry—"

Samantha's stomach clenched, but she couldn't tell whether it was from hunger or fear. "Wait a minute. You just said you were asked to leave the force. Is that why your old buddy at the station was so quick to say there wasn't much he could do?"

"No, I don't think so. There truly isn't much that can be done. But I was going to make contact after I'd gotten settled in. Pave the way with some buffalo wings. Your predicament just forced me there a little sooner." He glanced out the window then back to her, a glint of irritation in his eyes. "Do you think I don't remember anything of my training or my experience as an officer? I tried to tell you that there was nothing that could be done right now, but you didn't want to believe me."

"Why should I have trusted you? If I remember correctly, you were asked to leave the school. Something happened. I don't suppose you'd care to fill me in on that story."

Reid swallowed hard, his Adam's apple bobbing up and down. Samantha didn't care for asking such pointed questions, but her security, and Lily's, was at stake.

"I used to have a bit of a problem with anger. I was mad at everyone and everything back then. When I started law school, I was still angry with the police department for what I thought they had done to me. Then at the law school it seemed, to me at least, that the professors were grossly unfair. One day near the end of the first year, our torts professor pushed me too hard during one class. I couldn't come up with the answer to his question in the time he expected, and he started berating me in front of the class." He paused and fingered the Jeep's upholstery. "I lost it. I yelled at the professor. Turns out that's a cardinal sin in graduate education. It's not something I'm proud of and most of the time I'm pretty good at leaving it where it belongs. In the past."

In the past. Samantha fought down the urge to touch his hand. After Reid had left the law school, rumors had floated back that he had changed somehow, that another incident had led him to a turning point, but Samantha hadn't known him well enough to be in the circle of acquaintances who kept up with him. He'd been gone, and it just simply hadn't concerned her. Now she prayed that those rumors had been true and he had changed for the better. She let herself reach out to touch his arm, a gesture of comfort that ended up comforting her.

"But apparently you finished school. Elsewhere?"

A shadow of something, perhaps an elusive

memory from his past, flitted across his face. He slowly drew his attention back to her, as if being summoned from a distant thought. "Yes."

Samantha waited for more, but apparently a one-word answer was all she was going to get. Either Reid was one of those strong, silent types, or he didn't want to confess his sins, no matter how good for the soul that was supposed to be.

"What type of law do you practice? You must have a job lined up if you just drove in today. You start on Monday?"

More silence followed by a loud swallowing sound. "Uh, family law is my preference." He shifted in his seat. "Guardianships, adoptions, maybe a little of wills and trusts. And no job. I'm thinking of starting my own practice."

Heat crept over Samantha, but at least her inflamed cheeks would be hidden by the late twilight. So that was yet another reason for his evasion.

Invasion. Into her legal territory.

Lily's face shone in the fast-food joint's neon lights as thunder rumbled through the Jeep. Of course, there was nothing stopping her from getting out of the vehicle and walking Lily into the restaurant. She could call someone, anyone, from in there and ditch Reid completely. But the thugs were still out there, looking for her and Lily. Despite Reid's reputation as a defiant rule breaker, he had protected them so far. If she left, then what would she do? Who would protect her?

She tapped her first two fingers against her lips. She would stick with Reid, if he would have her.

"Sam, I am about to keel over from hunger back here." Lily's whine filled the Jeep, forcing Samantha to concentrate on the more immediate problem. Hunger. "Just give me some money, and I'll grab a burger or maybe some chicken tenders. You want anything?"

"Young lady, you are not leaving this vehicle." Egad, the tone in her voice sounded just like her mother's. When had that happened? She wanted to be a cool mom. A friend more than a dictator, benevolent or otherwise.

She glanced at Reid, but he only shrugged his shoulders. *Thanks a lot.*

"Come on, Sam. A ketchup packet? A little thingy of salt?"

"Not here." She put the Jeep into Reverse and pulled out of the spot. Then she turned it in the opposite direction the black SUV had gone a few minutes before.

Reid didn't say anything, so she headed up

the main street another block and turned into another fast-food burger place.

"Is it safe to go through the drive-through?" She turned her gaze to the rearview mirror, fighting back the urge to rake her hand through her hair.

Reid scanned the streets surrounding the restaurant. "I think it'll be fine. While we eat, we can figure out what to do next."

Samantha turned toward the squawk box and ordered two adult meals and a kid's meal plus a milk shake. The shake would be a treat for Lily, something to keep her mind off their current predicament, and maybe Samantha could get a few sips of chocolate, as well. It wouldn't be as calming as solid dark chocolate melting on her tongue, but desperate times called for desperate measures.

A few minutes later, they sat in the back of the parking lot, hidden behind the brick Dumpster enclosure, munching burgers and savoring the hot, salty aroma of French fries. Lily rummaged through the colorful sack her meal had come in and extracted the clear plastic bag that contained the prize. She ripped it open and popped a pair of sunglasses with rectangular frames onto her nose.

With darkness encroaching, Samantha could just barely make out the storm clouds that still hovered in the sky. "Lily, it's too dark for sunglasses. Why don't you put those away until tomorrow?"

"These aren't just sunglasses, Sam." She turned away from them to look out her side window. "There's a little mirror that lets me see what's behind me. For spying. Cool, huh?"

Yeah, supercool. Lily would be playing spy now for the next month and a half. Reid was apparently nonplussed as he took another big bite of his hamburger.

Lily giggled. "You have a bit of mayonnaise on your chin, Mr. Palmer. I can see it in my spy mirror."

"Since we're getting to know each other so well, you might as well call me Reid." Reid swiped at his face with a napkin. "And thanks for the heads-up." He held out his fist, and Lily bumped it with her own.

"No, no. There's no call for that." The last thing Samantha needed was for Lily to get chummy with a hothead like Reid Palmer. But would a hothead act like that with a ten-year-old, joking and not caring about mayo on his face? She sipped her drink, the coolness averting her attention from Reid and back to the decisions at hand. "Thank you so much for your assistance, Reid. You've been most helpful. Can we go home now?"

FIVE

"Home? Not advisable." Reid opened his backseat door. "And I think I better drive."

Samantha puffed hair out of her face, but she opened the driver's-side door and stalked around the front of the Jeep to climb into the front passenger seat. "If we can't go home, then where?"

"Not only would it be inappropriate to invite you to my place, but I don't even have a place. There were a couple of leads for apartments to rent from the newspaper I was going to check out this afternoon, but I arrived in town a little later than I wanted, and then an unfortunate accident took over the rest of my day. It's too late now to go knocking on a stranger's door." He pointed a stare at her. "What about your family? Parents? Siblings?"

He had dodged her questions to some extent so far. After all, who wanted to lay out all their sordid past for someone else's evaluation? He had worked with the officers at HHPD for several years, and they didn't even know the reason he rarely saw his father or how his mother had died. But with what he remembered and what he had seen tonight of the tenacious Samantha Callahan, he could be sure that if he spent much more time with her, there would be further interrogation.

She tore at a fingernail. "Out of town. Or unavailable."

He clicked his seat belt into place, the clacking of metal in the catch echoing throughout the silence of the Jeep. Whoever had come up with the statistic that women said twelve thousand words a day compared to men's five thousand obviously hadn't met Samantha. Her quietness should have been comfortable for him, yet it was oddly unnerving. He shifted in his seat, seeking a comfortable position. None was to be found.

Perhaps another tactic would elicit some helpful information. "We ought, also, to be thinking of who might be trying to kidnap you and Lily. That could help us put an end to being on the run. Does he want just Lily or both of you?"

"From what I saw at the church and the way he looked at me, I would guess he wants us both. If he wanted just Lily, couldn't he have grabbed her and stashed her away before I got there?"

"Sounds logical. But that doesn't necessarily make the situation any better."

Samantha turned in her seat, a softening shadowing her eyes. "Lily, honey, how's your arm? Where that guy grabbed you?"

Lily slurped on the shake, drawing out the last few drops. "It's all right, I guess. No biggie. But I sure don't want that to happen again."

"We're going to do our best to keep it from happening again."

We? Did that mean Samantha was going to stick around and let him help her? "It seems clear that whoever this is doesn't want you dead. You said he shot out your back windshield. If he's any good with a weapon, and we should assume that he is for our own safety, he could have hit either of you. But he didn't."

"That was my conclusion, as well." She paused. "Of course, now we're here with you, and he may not care about killing you."

"Yes." That disturbing thought had worried its way into the forefront of his thinking, and he didn't care to dwell on that probability.

"Kill you?" Lily asked from the backseat. "Seriously?"

Reid pivoted to meet her wide eyes. "We just need to be careful." No sense in getting the girl more scared that she probably already was. "Careful is always good."

"You never did tell me if you had a gun." That girl was a smarty-pants who didn't miss a thing.

"Well—" he aimed his attention back to Samantha "—any ideas who could be behind this? You don't recognize the guy who tried to grab you, so it's possible he's a hired thug. Is there any event or relationship from your past or present that could drive someone to this kind of action?"

Samantha pinched her lips, deep in thought. Several moments later, she shook her head. "No idea whatsoever."

"What about ransom?"

Lily poked her face in between the front seats. "What's ransom?"

"It means that someone could want to hold you or Samantha as their captive until you or someone pays them a certain amount of money. Usually a large, almost exorbitant, amount."

"*Exorbitant?* I like that word, Mr. Palmer. Does it mean an amount that's really, really big?"

This girl just got better and better. He hadn't gone through law school learning to question and defend and write briefs without acquiring some appreciation for word choice. "You got it."

Samantha pointed a stare at him that nearly pushed him out the door. Okay, he got the message. Apparently he wasn't supposed to get friendly with the kid. "As interesting as your ransom idea is, Reid—" she could have stabbed him with the force of her enunciation "—I just can't see it. Lily has a trust from her father's death, but it's not a large amount by any stretch of the imagination. I have some savings, but nothing significant. There are certainly bigger and wealthier targets. In fact, I shouldn't even use the word *wealthier* in that sentence. That implies that I or Lily have some wealth to begin with. It's funny how so many people think that lawyers are rich. But not all of us are."

Reid calculated what was in his checking and savings as well as what was in his wallet, and he had to agree. "What about family members who could be forced to pay a ransom amount?"

"My sister and I share the practice, so I know she wouldn't have much more than me. When my father left my mother, he nearly left her destitute. She wouldn't have anything to pay."

Reid swiped his hand through his hair. He

could almost hear the ding in his mind as long-forgotten pieces came together. "Wait a minute. What's your father's name?"

Samantha narrowed her gaze at him. She had probably figured out where his question was leading. "Thomas Callahan."

"You mean *the* Thomas Callahan, one of the most well-known and well-paid divorce attorneys in the Indianapolis area?"

"Unfortunately, yes. It's not a pretty thing when a prestigious divorce lawyer leaves his own wife." She pressed her hand to her chest as if the heart palpitations caused by the betrayal were still fresh.

Her expression was so pitiful Reid wanted to slide to the edge of his seat and take her in his arms, and whisper sweet comfort to her. But there was nothing worse he could do at this juncture, for her safety or his. In fact, the sooner this whole situation was resolved and he was removed from Samantha's presence, the better. He couldn't risk attachment, not with his history and the statistics to prove his genetic tendencies toward anger.

Before he could respond, Samantha killed that idea. "If these bad guys have done their research, they should know that my father would most likely not pay a ransom. We haven't spoken much over the years. When we do, it's rather curt. And we haven't been in contact at all in over a year."

"What about Lily? Who in her past would have money to pay a ransom?" Reid glanced at the backseat. Lily wore her spy sunglasses and was stroking her long ponytail, pulling it off to the side as if trying to see it in the mirror in the glasses.

Samantha picked at an invisible piece of lint on her skirt. "When she was only three, her mother died. So it's been just her and her dad for several years. I got to know her at church and became a sort of substitute mother for her. Her father was killed in a hit-and-run not long ago, but at least he had set up a will that appointed me as her guardian." She squinted at the dark sky and the clouds hovering outside her window. "Can we talk about this on the way to my condo? Surely we can at least pick up some clothes and necessary items before the rain starts."

Reid sagged in his seat, his ankle holster pressed into his leg. Perhaps just a few moments to run into her place would be all right. He turned the key in the ignition and checked his rearview mirror.

Lily sat in the middle of the backseat, clutching the purple backpack, a tear escaping from underneath her sunglasses.

* * *

Finally, Samantha was making some progress in her reasoning with Reid. Maybe once they got to her condo and all was well, he would see that she could stay there without problem.

Maybe she would be convinced of that, as well…especially since there was no place else to run.

At her instruction, Reid pulled out of the parking lot and turned right.

"Are you familiar with the Maple Grove Condominiums on the east side of town?"

Reid turned to smile at her. "It's been a while since I've been in Heartwood Hill. Several years. I'll need directions."

Even in the dark, Samantha could see a shadow of whiskers beginning to cover his jaw. She swallowed down the lump growing in her throat. She had to admit that Reid was an attractive man, but she couldn't account for her sudden desire for him to find her home pleasing. When was the last time she had dusted? Had she left dishes in the sink that morning? Did she have enough coffee to offer him a cup?

She pinched her own leg to punish herself for even thinking such thoughts. Someone with Reid's reputation would never be interested in the coziness and pleasures of home. Nor would she want him there. She and Lily were doing just fine by themselves.

She pointed to the next stoplight. "Turn left up there."

"So what else can you tell me about Lily's father?"

"I told you about all I know. The driver was never found, so we don't know who hit his car. Lily came home with me after seeing her father at the hospital, and she's been with me ever since."

"So he didn't die on impact?"

"No. She got to spend a little bit of time with him. It was good to say that goodbye, but bad to have to say it. You know what I mean?"

"Yeah. I do."

A catch in his voice touched something deep inside Samantha. Even the tall, strong and quiet Reid Palmer had some difficulty with his background. Samantha checked their location. "In here, at the subdivision sign. I'm in the third house on the left." Whatever more it was that was bothering him, she couldn't dwell on that now. Probably never. She had a child to protect, her first priority.

Reid drove slowly, sweeping his gaze over the other houses and down the side streets. "What did her father do? For a living?"

"He was an accountant with that big manu-
facturing company on the north side of Indy.
Why?"

"Just searching for information that might
help us figure out who's after you and Lily."

Samantha sniffed. "I didn't know a lot of the
details, but accountant sounded like a pretty
dreary job to me. I can't imagine that has anything to do with our present difficulty."

He idled past the house and turned right at
the next street.

"Where are we going? You passed it."

"I'm circling and double-checking." He
leaned forward and peered past her, in between
the houses that backed onto hers. "There was
only one car parked on the street, and no one
was in it. I think we're okay."

Reid pulled up in the driveway and cut the
headlights. Lily fidgeted in the backseat but
stilled when he held up a hand. "We'll sit here
for a moment and check it out."

The structure was cloaked in darkness, even
more so with the thunder-boomers blotting
out the nighttime stars. Samantha sat in the
eerie silence and let her gaze dart around the
yard. Everything seemed in place. Not a single
flower appeared to be trampled, although she
couldn't see all the beds in the dark. "Looks
fine to me," she whispered in Reid's direction.

"It doesn't seem that anyone's around, but it's hard to tell from the exterior. Let's go in, but be watchful and stay behind me." He leaned over the steering wheel and pulled up his pant leg, retrieving the weapon from the holster fastened to his lower leg. "And keep it quiet. Not even a whisper."

Lily lunged against the back of the seat. "I knew it! You do have a gun." Her hoarse whisper whipped through Samantha's hair.

"Whoa." Samantha scooted to the edge of her seat near the door. She'd never been close to a gun before. "You have a gun?"

"Yeah. What police officer, even former, wouldn't be armed?"

"You have a permit for that thing?"

"Of course. And in Indiana it's called a license."

Samantha tucked a loose lock of hair behind her ear with a trembling hand. "Stay back, Lily. Let Mr. Palmer handle this." She should have figured a former police officer would carry a weapon, but she hadn't been prepared for her innocent ward's sudden interest in firearms.

"I'm not going to touch it, Sam. And I know better than to stand in front of it. I just want to look at it…from here." Samantha couldn't quite tell in the darkness, but Lily probably executed a classic eye roll as only a ten-year-old could.

Reid swung his door open and motioned for Samantha and Lily to do the same. He slowly pushed it closed without latching it, and Samantha softly closed hers as well, grabbing Lily's before the girl could slam it shut.

As they approached the door, Samantha uttered a prayer thanking the Lord for sending such a tall, broad-shouldered protector. She hated to put him in the line of fire, but at least he could fire back.

He nudged the butt of his gun against the door, and it swung open. Someone had been there for sure. There was no way she would leave the door hanging open when she went to work. Besides, she usually left through the garage. The front door was only opened when she or her sister, with whom she shared the condo, were expecting guests.

But one glimpse inside was all she needed to know she wouldn't be staying there anytime soon.

Reid stepped in first, but Samantha peeked around him. She flew her hand to cover her gasp at the utter destruction that waited her inside her home.

Every single picture had been thrown down from the wall. Holes a couple of inches wide pockmarked the walls. Her collection of houseplants that resided near the front window had been tipped over. Scratch marks tore through the piles of dirt on the carpet. Even the sofa cushions had been cut open, their stuffing pulled out. Only her chenille throw, her favorite accompaniment to an afternoon of reading, remained untouched.

Lily grabbed Samantha's arm, gasping for air as she surveyed the damage. Her face shone pale in the dark house, and Samantha pulled Lily's hands together and cupped them over her mouth. If Lily didn't calm down, she'd hyperventilate, and they didn't need the ten-year-old passing out to complicate an already complicated situation.

Samantha drew Lily close, into the crook of her arm, and stepped toward Reid. There was no telling who was still in the house, and the best place she could think to be was near the guy with the weapon. She stumbled on a couple of books lying haphazardly on the floor and lurched toward Reid, grasping his arm to steady herself. He flinched slightly but didn't move away. She pulled closer to the comfort of his strength, and the three picked a way through the room and into the kitchen.

He held out his phone to her. "Call nine-one-one," he whispered. "And stick close."

If it was possible, the kitchen was even worse. Every container in the pantry had been opened and seemingly dumped on the floor. Cabinet doors hung open, the contents splayed across the shelves. Even the ice maker had been emptied into the sink.

Both Samantha and her twin Mallory's room had dresser drawers opened and contents dumped. Her poor mattress had been slashed and the fabric torn apart. She reached to upright a perfume bottle on the chest of drawers, but Reid's hoarse whisper stilled her.

"Don't touch anything. We should call the police. They ought to dust for fingerprints, but considering what we know about this guy's MO, he, or they, probably wore gloves."

"MO?" Lily's voice squeaked in the hush.

"*Modus operandi.* It's Latin. Means 'method of working.' We've seen that these guys act like professionals. Professionals would wear gloves to make sure they don't leave fingerprints."

"Because the police can identify someone by their fingerprints."

"Exactly."

Samantha squeezed Reid's arm. "Do you really think we should be talking?"

"Let's keep it to a whisper, but I think they're gone. They probably came here first this afternoon, even before they found Lily at the church."

Samantha's heart thumped and bumped in her chest, as if it were a wild animal trying to break free. Should she be comforted that the thugs likely weren't here anymore? Or should she be even more panicky at the idea that her home had been in this violated condition, the front door open, all evening?

Suddenly, Lily jerked loose from Samantha's arm and took off down the hall. "My room!"

Samantha's glance collided with Reid's look of alarm. She ran toward Lily's voice, Reid close on her heels. As she entered the doorway, lightning flashed in the window, illuminating the entire space for a split second. As the resulting thunder rumbled across the room, shaking the house to its very foundation, she stared at the spots in her vision, trying to black out the image of Lily's room in complete destruction.

Curtains were pulled off the window. The mattress was a shambles, and even the box springs had been cut open. Drawers had been upended, the contents spewed all over the floor. The closet doors had been ripped off the track. It looked as if someone had stood in front of the closet and systematically pulled everything off the hangers and the shelves in a search for something. Even the rug had been pulled up around the edges of the room.

They had been looking for something. But what?

Lily turned to Samantha and burrowed against her front. Samantha wrapped her arms around the girl in what she prayed was a comforting embrace even as she tried in vain to stifle the sobs that bellowed up from deep within.

Silence engulfed the trio for a moment before the long-anticipated rain finally began. The first drops hit gently, a soothing melody against the roof, until it fell harder and harder. Samantha rubbed Lily's back, searching for God in the storm. If only the deluge could bring a cleansing of the soul and wash away the grief and disruption that had been the girl's constant companion.

Reid broke the quiet with a throat clearing. "Looks as if they spent most of their time in this room. I'm guessing they're looking for something they think she has or something she knows. But they trashed the whole place, so they might think that you know something about it, as well. I would also guess they didn't find it, since now they're after you two."

"What, though?" Samantha surveyed the destruction of the room again. "What could they possibly want?"

"That's the question, isn't it? Could be money, but that wouldn't explain why they're coming after you. Maybe particular documents, a computer file, valuables. There's no way to know for sure."

He picked up a scrapbook that had been tossed onto the floor. Lily had pasted a photo of herself with her father on the cover. Reid thumbed through it, revealing pages hanging askew. Little pockets and flaps Lily had glued in to keep her mementos of her father had been torn out and littered on the floor. It seemed that no one page of the scrapbook had gone untouched. "Perhaps it has something to do with her father?"

Samantha released one arm around Lily to press on the bridge of her nose. As she had grown to know Lily, Samantha had sensed that the girl needed an anchor in her life, especially with her father working so much and still grieving the death of his wife. But she had no idea Lily might carry a secret with her, let alone one that was dangerous.

Reid tapped her hand, and she was startled to see his phone there. The shock of the destruction was still rippling through her, and she had completely forgotten the call. She quickly dialed as Reid whispered, "Be thinking about what to grab to be gone at least a few days."

"Nine-one-one. What's your emergency?"

The answer sounded loud in her ear, especially after all their whispering, and she scrambled to voice her problem. "Break-in. My house."

"Are you in any danger?"

She stepped closer to Reid, soaking up the energy and safety that radiated from him. "I don't think so."

"What is your exact location?"

She rattled off her address, satisfaction settling over her like a comfortable shirt, a sensation she welcomed as she stood in the midst of destruction.

At Reid's direction, Samantha grabbed an overnight bag at the back of her closet that had been untouched and began collecting a few personal items the police wouldn't need to examine. Apparently, he had been right. She and Lily couldn't go home. They were on the run now, but at least they had Reid for protection.

There was no one else to trust.

SIX

Reid rubbed his hands together as he surveyed the damage. For all his years on the force, he hadn't seen much like this. Heartwood Hill was a sleepy little suburb, and not much happened. Whatever was going on, it was serious.

Samantha finished the call and handed the phone back. "He said he'll send a unit."

Who would be on duty tonight? And why did that wondering strike trepidation into his soul? He had only good things to prove about himself. Changes that he prayed would last for the long-term, with God's help. But if his reception by Cody early that evening had been any indication, the path to renewed and improved relationships with his former police brothers was going to be steep and rocky. It was yet another reason why a prosecutor's position wouldn't work. Excellent relationships with law enforcement were an absolute necessity.

Samantha moved into the bathroom and began filling her bag with her toothbrush and toothpaste.

"I'll wait outside while you finish up. Fill in the officers when they arrive."

She nodded her assent, probably all she could muster right now.

Outside, he surveyed the perimeter, but the roughnecks were long gone. Upon closer inspection, he saw that the slider at the back patio had been jimmied. With no bar in the track to prevent the door from sliding open, the thugs had easily broken the lock and gained access.

A car engine sounded around the front of the house, and Reid jogged around the side, his heart thumping in time to his steps. He stopped at the corner, relief flooding him. It was Derek, a good guy who had been a good friend, and a rookie he didn't know.

Derek caught sight of him and stared for a moment, then a grin spread across his face. "Reid? What are you doing here?"

Reid approached, uncertain of the protocol, but Derek grabbed him into a manly, back-thumping hug. "Don't know if news ever filtered back, but I'm a lawyer now. Drove into town today to look for an apartment and a job, but got rear-ended by Samantha Callahan." He gestured toward the home. "Long story short, this is her house. B and E, and it's torn up pretty good. Seems someone is after her and the ten-year-old girl she's guardian to."

The rookie grabbed a case from the trunk and approached Reid to shake his hand.

"This is Gizmo." Derek shot a wink to Reid. "He just joined us a couple months ago. He is…uh…young and energetic."

"Weren't we all at one point in time?" Reid smiled, although his mood did not feel as light as what he hoped his expression was.

"Good to meet you, sir."

Sir? When did he get to be a *sir*? It was true that Reid had lived a lot of life and committed many wrongs in his thirty-three years, sins that laid a weight on him and aged him. But he wasn't ready to pull up the afghan and sit in the rocker yet. God had given him a new life, hadn't He? A second chance? He plastered his smile back in place and simply muttered, "Good to meet you, too."

The officers weren't at the house long and didn't express much hope in any evidence left behind. They took Samantha and Lily's statements, and Reid filled them in on what he had seen when they arrived. Photos were snapped and fingerprints lifted. Derek promised he would take point on the investigation, and would let Reid know what forensics found, if anything. But an hour later, they were gone with only an offer to drive through the subdivision every now and then to keep an eye on neighborhood activity, and a suggestion from Derek that he and Reid should meet for coffee sometime.

Samantha stood next to him in the kitchen, looking lost. "So what now?"

Yes, indeed. What now? The obvious thing was to avoid detection while figuring out who was after Samantha and Lily and why, and then bring the full force of the law down on their heads. But how to avoid detection? Heartwood Hill was only so big. To leave town would be to leave the police department that was now, at least superficially, familiar with the case.

"We go." Sounds of drawers opening and closing sounded from Lily's room. The poor girl was probably trying to straighten everything, make sense of the situation. "You can't stay here, not with those guys still at large."

Samantha hugged herself, and Reid shoved his hands into his pockets to quell the desire to hug her himself. What had gotten into him? Attachment in any way, shape or form was completely inadvisable and would only result in disappointment for the both of them.

But he couldn't just ditch them. Before he'd turned to God, he had known plenty of guys who would have just dropped Samantha and the kid off at their house, even when it had been trashed, and taken off. They wouldn't want to be burdened by someone with a ten-year-old girl, let alone someone in trouble and needing help. Fun had been the name of the game. Before he'd turned to God, he had been one of those guys. But the new Reid Palmer couldn't leave her. Not only because he needed a new and improved reputation in Heartwood Hill and a good working relationship with the Callahan twins, but also...just because.

Because there was something comforting yet energizing about being with Samantha. Because in the short time they'd been in the Jeep together, he'd realized how lonely being alone can be.

Because he wanted desperately to be a gentleman. He felt it within himself, bubbling up like a hot spring despite the fact that his father had never modeled gentlemanly behavior, and now was his chance to make good on it. Because he wanted to prove that he had escaped his past, his father's disposition that even now coursed through the blood in Reid's own veins. Reid couldn't ever risk a relationship, but he would sleep better at night, be more comfortable in his skin, if he proved to himself that the angry, rabble-rousing days were over. That he was not his father.

He would never be his father.

"Reid?"

Samantha's worried tone broke his reverie, and for the first time in his life, he wished he carried change in his pocket, something to keep his hands busy, away from Samantha's trembling shoulders. If there couldn't be a relationship, there ought not be affection.

He shook his head to clear the thoughts. "Neither of us has a place now, so we stay at a hotel, at least for tonight. Maybe some sleep will help us figure this out. Gather your stuff and Lily, and let's get out of here. And make sure to bring Lily's scrapbook about her father. Just in case it has something to do with all this."

Back in the Jeep, Reid turned out of Samantha's subdivision and headed back toward the commercial strip of town. In the darkness, he suppressed a wry smile. He had been concerned that Heartwood Hill would have changed so much in his absence that he would have to learn it all over again, adding more stress to his reentry. But this chauffeuring was certainly reacquainting him quickly.

A number of hotels stretched near the interstate ramps, and he pulled into the cheapest motel and drove around back, parking the Jeep but letting it idle.

Samantha's gaze darted around the dark exterior. "Is this where we're staying?"

Reid surveyed the only entrance to that part of the parking lot. "No. I'm waiting to see if someone's following us."

A full ten minutes later, no one else had nosed into that secluded spot, and as he pulled around front, all the vehicles were the same as when he had pulled in. He turned right onto the main highway and circled around the fast-food place they'd been at earlier, then turned into the priciest of the hotels. In this parking spot, he turned off the engine and cut the lights.

"Do you see anyone?" Samantha had scrunched down in her seat.

"No. I think we're good."

Then he selected a middle-range place to stay and pulled into the parking garage. The garage seemed a bit fancy for such a small suburb, but now Reid was grateful for the added protection. This hotel wouldn't eat up his cash but would be clean and stocked with fresh towels. Breakfast in the morning would be nice, too, since his usual fare only included a cup of joe. Samantha and Lily accompanied him to the front desk, Lily clutching her pillow. He secured two adjoining rooms and paid with the rest of his cash. He'd have to find an ATM tomorrow.

Lily had staggered down the hallway half-asleep. As Lily headed to the shower, Reid instructed Samantha to put her in the bed farthest from the door. That would leave Samantha the bed close to the door, just in case, and he would be right next door.

He stepped into his room to give the girls some privacy, then returned later as Samantha tucked the blanket around Lily, whose soft breathing whispered between them. "It'll be all right, won't it?" She gazed up at him, questions and doubts clouding her blue eyes.

"Everything will look better in the morning." He hated it, but the platitude his mother used to feed him after one of his father's brawls seemed the easiest way out at the moment.

Without a word or any indication of whether or not she believed him, she closed the door between the two rooms.

With only the bathroom light filtering into his room, Reid sat on the edge of his bed and removed his shoes, leaving them at the ready next to the bedside table. He lay on top of the covers, fully dressed. Sleep would not come easy that night, if at all. Too much was at stake.

He hated to bother her, but he needed more information about Lily's father. He padded to her door and knocked quietly. "Samantha? You awake?" he whispered.

A few moments later, she opened the door and leaned against the doorjamb. "Yeah."

"What else do you know about Lily's father?"

"Like I said, he was an accountant, but I don't know at what level, if any. He was always so quiet that I never really got to know him. At first, I thought it was grief for his wife. But I think that was just him. Quiet, but still strong. You know what I mean? He wasn't pushy with his opinions, but he didn't waver from his beliefs."

"What about friends? Acquaintances?"

"I don't know. I only spent a little bit of time with him, not much because I was mostly with Lily. I also saw him when I picked her up or dropped her off or at church. The last time I picked her up, right before he died, he had just given her a beautiful heart-shaped key chain. He didn't usually give gifts like that, but I thought he just wanted her to carry a key to the house. Eventually, she gave it to me for safekeeping." She rubbed her eyes and stifled a yawn. "I'm sorry. What were you asking about? Oh, yeah, friends of Lily's father. No, he was usually alone, working on his computer or reading a book that looked computerish. Boring, so I didn't pay much attention."

"Did you ever see what was on his computer?"

"No." She exhaled loudly into the dark room. "Can we talk about this later? I don't want to wake up Lily. She needs her sleep, and the last thing we need tomorrow is a cranky, sleep-deprived adolescent."

"Sure. Night."

She closed the door without a word, and soon her sleepy breathing sounded louder than Lily's.

Reid lay back down and tucked his hands behind his head, staring at the sliver of light coming from the bathroom. What an odd predicament he found himself in, and on his first night back in town. Sharing adjoining hotel rooms, weapon at the ready, with a former law-school classmate and her ward? What did the Lord have in store for him next? Because it sure was an unusual way to form an amicable working relationship with a local lawyer.

What seemed like moments later, Reid startled at the sound of footsteps outside the door. A glance at the clock revealed he had slept for about an hour. All seemed quiet behind Samantha and Lily's door. He lay still, holding his breath, waiting for another sound.

There. More footsteps right outside the door.

Then a slight rattle of the doorknob, like someone was jimmying it or trying to insert a key card.

Reid shot up, slipped his feet into his shoes and tied his laces. He raced quietly to the window and pulled the side of the curtain back just enough to peek down at his Jeep.

In the blackness of the night, a dark shadow, barely perceptible with only a smidgen of moonlight, peered into the backseat of his vehicle. One thug was checking his Jeep. Another was at his door. His advantage was that the thug at the door didn't know they had two rooms.

Despite his police training, his heart leaped into his throat. It was different when it was personal.

"Samantha." His voice was a hoarse whisper as he tapped at her door. He prayed he wasn't too loud.

The jiggling continued at his door.

He heard movement on the other side, and the door slowly opened. "Samantha, they're here. We need to go."

He stepped to his door to the hallway noiselessly, holding his breath. His heart beat so loudly he feared the thug on the other side of the door would hear. Their best plan was to make the guy think they were all in that room, so silence was absolutely critical. He grabbed his bag and placed it inside Samantha's room. Then he stepped through and gently closed the adjoining door. He assumed a position behind the door and flicked out the light. Total darkness consumed them.

The door lock clicked on his room door, and someone from the outside depressed the handle. With a slight scrape across the carpet, the door swung open.

Reid held his breath as he waited for the footsteps to cross completely into the room. As soon as the man completed as many steps as Reid figured it would take to reach the bed, he tossed a whisper to Samantha and Lily, who huddled by their room door. "Now!"

Samantha threw the door open, halting it just before it hit the doorstop. He stepped up behind them and motioned for them to go in front. "Stairs! To the left!"

They ran for the stairwell. Reid blinked in the bright light of the hallway. Surely the thug's eyes wouldn't be able to adjust between light and dark and then light again so quickly that he could catch up. Samantha popped open the stairwell door and barreled through. Reid brought up the rear, but before the door closed them in the stairwell, he heard the hotel room door open again. The man would be close upon them in a moment.

Samantha longed to stop and rub her calves. Leaping out of a sound sleep and into action was not easy for the body or the mind. She struggled to process what time it might be, but all she glimpsed outside the stairwell windows was utter darkness broken only by the lights of nearby businesses.

A door opened and closed somewhere behind them. "Faster," Reid urged them. He was following close behind, as Samantha led. Shouldn't Reid be in front? What if a bad guy waited just outside the first-floor door? But what if the bad guy behind them caught up? Reid had a gun, so maybe he could protect them. Either way, she yearned to be at home in her bed, free from men with their weapons.

"Head for the superstore across the lot." Reid's voice sounded closer behind now.

Open twenty-four hours. Bright lights. Employees and shoppers. That sounded like a good plan.

Samantha risked a glance back. Lily wore a wide-awake expression of intensity, not even breathing heavily after their rapid descent from their third-floor hotel room. She was in good shape for all her wear and tear, but no child should have to go through this. The sooner they could get to safety, the better. Samantha hightailed it through the last door and hit the humidity at a run. She gasped to inhale the moist air, immediately slowed by the sogginess that hung still and heavy. But she pushed herself toward the big, bright supercenter, like a bug drawn to the light.

Lily caught up and jogged alongside her as they crossed the parking lot. Only a handful of cars littered the area, and Samantha prayed that the store was filled with night employees stocking the shelves. She slowed as they approached the front door, and she ran her hand down the front of her T-shirt to smooth the wrinkles. At least she had been able to change out of her business attire when they reached the hotel earlier that night, and Lily had been able to take a shower to wash away her day-camp stench.

The doors whooshed open, and blessedly cool air enveloped them. Reid stepped up next to her. She grasped Lily's hand and pulled her forward as they walked past the welcoming displays of summer treats. A couple of bored cashiers turned to watch them walk past.

"Slow. Slow." It was barely more than a grunt from Reid.

She dropped her pace immediately and

pasted what she hoped was a nonchalant expression on her face. She glanced at the end caps as they sauntered by. Her favorite brownie mix was on sale for an excellent price. Under normal circumstances, she would buy a box and enjoy time in the kitchen with Lily, then savor each delectable morsel while they watched an old favorite Fred Astaire movie.

These were anything but normal circumstances, though.

She glanced at Reid. Did he like brownies? Would that be his idea of an enjoyable evening? Dessert and a movie at home? Why was she even wondering about it? Her biggest priority right now was Lily. Lily was her responsibility, true. But it was difficult to keep her mind from wandering to the possibility of something with Reid. She couldn't quite grasp it, but there was a sense of security about him that she could get used to. A refuge in the storm.

Reid glanced behind them, then suddenly steered them down an aisle toward the toy and outdoor department. "He's here."

As he pushed her around the bend, Samantha sneaked a glance back. It was the same guy, complete with the cap and the dark sunglasses. Where was the other one? Was he waiting for them around the corner or for them to exit the building? Beads of perspiration sprang to her forehead, but she didn't dare to swipe them away for fear she would draw attention to herself.

Reid weaved them in and out of displays of children's shirts and women's socks until they stepped up to the bottom of an outdoor play set. The two-story, solid-wood structure sat on top of a shelving unit and rose above them almost to the ceiling. Reid arched his gaze up then turned to her. "We hide here until he's gone. Lily, take the top level and stay down. Behind the railing."

Samantha gawked at Lily climbing the shelves and hoisting herself up to the play set without help. "What? Are you serious? Is it sturdy?"

Reid surveyed up and down the aisle. "I'd rather get up there than stay down here and face the guy with the gun. What's your pick?" He threaded his fingers together and leaned down to make a step for her.

Fine. There really was no other option, and Lily was up to her perch already. It was a good choice. From their vantage point, they could probably see the thug move throughout the store, and they would know when he left.

The two of them barely fit side by side on the bottom level. She got on her knees and leaned down on her elbows, twisting a bit until she could see through the slats of the railing. It would be the perfect position for praying, if she wasn't so distracted by the softness of Reid's shirt against her arm or the clean, laundry-soap scent that emanated from him or the warm feeling of safety from his biceps resting against her shoulder.

Reid pointed through his slats. Samantha followed the line of sight until she spotted the thug in the shoe section. Her throat instantly went dry, and she swallowed hard over the lump in her throat. No gun was visible, but he was quite far away. He was also probably smart enough to conceal it in the store so he wouldn't draw attention to himself. He stopped next to the sale rack of flip-flops and let his gaze sweep upward and around the store.

Samantha jerked down behind the play set's railing. "Lily, down," she whispered.

Samantha turned her head toward Reid. She would be able to judge by his reaction if the thug saw them, and that would be a lot easier to handle than making direct eye contact with the guy who was after them.

Reid shifted a knee, and the wood structure creaked under the weight of his large frame.

Uh-oh. That didn't bode well for their outcome. A shiver stair-stepped up Samantha's spine. What if the bad guy heard and found them? What if the entire play set crashed down under Reid's weight? What if...? Samantha wanted to rub the start of a headache away from her temple but didn't dare to move a hand. All these what-ifs would drive her crazy.

She sympathized with the guy, though. He probably felt like a sardine squeezed into a tiny can. What she couldn't figure out was what was in it for him. Why did he keep protecting them? It would be so easy for him just to turn her and Lily over to the thugs. Or just dump them at home. He could even have lost them in the store. So why take these risks?

Did he just love brandishing his weapon, or the idea of rescuing the damsel in distress? Because the way she remembered it she was doing just fine until she rear-ended his Jeep. She and Lily were escaping by their own power and with God's help. Or was he trying to get on her good side since he planned to set up a law practice that would compete directly with hers? Either way, the sooner this whole problem was resolved, the better.

Reid's expression didn't change as he watched the thug out in the store, so Samantha risked a look. It took a moment to find him, but he was headed toward the tires and car batteries and oil-change station. A moment later, Reid jostled her with his elbow. "He's gone.

Let's get out of here before I can't straighten my legs."

She tapped on the underside of the top level of the play set. When Lily poked her head out at the ladder, Samantha waved her down. Once they were safely on the floor, Reid led them through the aisle of badminton games, volleyballs and weight sets toward a back room.

Samantha grabbed his arm to stop him. "Shouldn't we go back out the front?"

Reid's cheek muscle ticked. He met Lily's gaze. She shrugged, wearing an I-don't-know-what-her-problem-is expression.

He grabbed Samantha's hand and pushed the door open. He'd protected them thus far, so why did she question him? She squeezed his hand, hoping he understood it as the apology she meant it to be.

A long, gray hallway with storage rooms on all sides stretched before them. He paused once they were all inside and looked up and down.

"Now what?" Lily's voice squeaked in the cavernous space.

"We find an exit."

A few yards down, they turned a corner. An exit sign glowed over a door at the end of that short hallway. Samantha exhaled a breath she had been holding as a burden lifted off her chest. They would be safe soon.

She pulled her hand away from Reid's and grasped Lily's. Lily was her concern, not Reid, and the more she remembered that, the better off they would all be. Lily curled her fingers around Samantha's hand, a clutching that sought safety and security. Samantha prayed that she would be able to provide that for the girl.

They were a few feet from the door, freedom in reach.

"Stop!" The strident voice echoed around the bare hallway. Lily let go of Samantha's hand to cover her ears.

Samantha glanced back. It was him. The man who had broken into their hotel room and then followed them into the store.

"Run!" Reid commanded, and her feet obeyed. "Get out."

She and Lily dashed past Reid. In her peripheral vision, she saw him turn and follow.

Lily grunted at Samantha's side, a step ahead.

At the door, she pushed it open and Lily ran through. As she jogged through, she turned to look back. The thug lumbered only two paces behind Reid.

Samantha moved aside as Reid stepped through the door. He swiveled around and grabbed the edge of the door, shoving it back toward the thug as he tried to step through. The heavy metal door collided with the thug's face with a resounding crack. He fell back and hit the floor. They watched for a moment, but the man didn't move.

"Whoa!" Fright tinged Lily's tone. "Is he dead?"

"No. Just unconscious." Reid stepped back into the building and felt the guy's neck for a pulse. Apparently satisfied, he straightened. "He'll be fine. He'll just have a bad headache when he wakes up." He looked back down the hallway. "I'm sure someone heard all that commotion. They'll be here to help him in a few moments and call the police. We can't stick around, though, with the other guy still looking for us."

He led them away from the building and closed the door gently behind them. The rough cement of the exterior wall of the supercenter scraped on Samantha's arms and legs as they hugged the back of the building all the way to the corner closest to the hotel. They dashed to a large stand of pines in between the two structures. Samantha peered between the trees, but cloud cover blocked the moonlight and she couldn't detect any movement around the outside of the hotel. Apparently, Reid was satisfied, and he shuttled them to the back corner of the hotel building. The storm continued to threaten, and a streak of lightning illuminated the parking garage.

In another moment, they were back at the Jeep, just as the rain finally let loose. Samantha hung back to make sure that Lily made it into the backseat, then she slid into the front and pulled the belt over herself. Reid slammed his door and jammed the key in the ignition. The moment the engine roared to life, Reid thrust it into Reverse and pulled out of the parking lot.

Once out on the highway, he headed back toward the center of town, windshield wipers running at full force. Samantha glanced at the speedometer. He drove just a few miles over the speed limit, probably so they wouldn't draw any attention.

She rotated in her seat to see Lily in the back. Lily's eyelids drooped, and her shoulders sagged. Lily had managed to get her seat belt secured, but now her head lolled with the swaying of the vehicle. Samantha's heart crept toward her throat as tears welled in her eyes. Awe swept over her again that God would trust such a precious soul to her care. She whispered a prayer for the girl who was probably still grieving the loss of her father. The girl Samantha hoped would call her Mom someday.

She swiveled back toward the front, halting as she stared at Reid's profile. Streetlights flashing across his face revealed a jaw set with determination, a determination she was glad was in their favor. Whatever was in Reid's past, it seemed he had mastered it. He was on her side and for that she was grateful. But would it be enough to overcome the guys who were after them?

With no idea where they were going and the rain falling strong and steady, it became abundantly clear that she had no other option than to trust.

SEVEN

It was exactly what he hadn't wanted to use: physical force. But what else could he have done?

Reid scrubbed a hand over his face. Light snoring sounded from the backseat, and a cursory glance at Samantha revealed her head bobbing to the rhythm of the drive. A light rain continued to patter on the roof of the Jeep, making good sleeping weather.

At least they were safe. Again. He had acted on instinct honed by training and experience and used just enough strength to subdue the guy temporarily but not hurt him permanently. He had reassured Samantha and Lily of that, but he could tell by the wary look that haunted the lines around her eyes that she wasn't accustomed to witnessing such action.

If he had to face the awful truth, it had repulsed even him. As the lights of a sleepy Heartwood Hill slowly flashed past, he wrestled yet again with the past he hadn't asked for and hadn't wanted. Would he ever have a healthy handle on life? Chances were poor for that, since his only brother hadn't been able to deal with the abuse of their childhood. In fact, he'd adopted their father's problems as his own and was currently serving time in the very same facility as their dad. Did they share a father-son cell? Some people could find humor in the midst of pain, but what about when the pain remained as raw as an open wound? It just didn't make any sense. And despite his current state of salvation, he still wore his past like a set of shackles around his ankles. Most days it seemed like a life sentence.

It was late, but Derek needed to be up to speed. Reid dialed his buddy, awakening him from sleep. It only took a minute to fill him in, then he hung up, satisfied that Derek was on it.

He surveyed all the mirrors but didn't see a tail as he drove through downtown and the south side of the suburb. If memory served, there was a ramshackle barn at the end of a country road a couple of turns off the highway. Probably some farmer owned it and didn't have the time or resources to either fix it up or tear it down. If it still stood, it would serve as a hiding spot, at least for the night. They were all desperate for some sleep, and apparently they would have to make their beds in his Jeep. He would be able to think more clearly in the morning with a few hours of sleep. At the very least, if they were discovered, they could make a quick getaway.

So far, so good. The dirt road seemed the same, albeit a bit muddy now, and the silhouette of the barn leaned precariously against what he could see of the night sky through the rain. He cut the headlights and the engine and stopped several yards off the highway, sitting in silence for many minutes. He checked his watch in the moonlight. Nearly two o'clock in the morning now. Not a single car zipped past. The night remained eerily silent, void of any activity or sound except the pitter-patter of the raindrops.

Confident they hadn't been followed, he started the vehicle again but left the lights off. As he continued toward the barn, the bumping of the rutted road jostled Samantha awake. Something startled her, perhaps the remembrance of their prior trouble, and she sat upright, her eyes wide as she surveyed their surroundings.

Reid touched her arm, an unexpected sensation of electricity in his fingertips. Her strawberry blond hair fell away from her face, revealing the freckle pattern traced across her nose. A catch in his chest made him anxious to soothe her and to settle her nerves. "We're fine. We're out in the country, and I'm pretty sure we haven't been followed."

She looked down at his hand on her arm and then turned eyes of sorrow and frustration toward him. Perhaps that look was because she was still trying to process where they were and what all had happened. Sleep could discombobulate a person's mind in the midst of a traumatic situation. But could it also have been a search for comfort and connection?

She cleared her throat. "Where are we going?"

"See that barn?" He nodded out the windshield and placed both hands on the steering wheel. "We're going to park behind it and catch some sleep. But I'm glad you're awake. We need to talk about what to do in the morning. I don't want to hang around once the sun comes up."

"Wait a minute. Sleep in the car?"

"Unless you have a better idea?"

She sat silent for a moment, chewing her bottom lip. When she didn't respond, Reid continued. "Those guys from the hotel and the store surely know my Jeep by now, so we're going to need to switch cars. I've been through a lot with this Jeep. It's in good condition and it's paid for. So I'm not eager to sell it and get something that may be unreliable. I don't think we have the time or opportunity for car shopping anyway. Yours, obviously, is out of commission."

"Thanks to you."

Reid gripped the steering wheel. That rear-ending was not his fault, but now was not the time to discuss it all over again. Samantha stared out the side window, her arms hugging her middle. She was grumpy from the upset in her life. Understandably so.

Reid swallowed down the desire to bite back. "I thought about a rental, but I don't think either of us has much money. I also don't want to risk a credit card charge, in case these guys after you and Lily have the ability to track us that way. Since I just drove into town, I don't have anyone I can call to borrow a car, especially in a situation that might get it banged up. What about you? You know anyone who would be willing to loan us a vehicle?"

A thick crop of corn stood tall about the barn as Reid pulled up behind it. The structure leaned as if it didn't have too many days left on this earth, and he prayed that it wouldn't fall down on them. He cracked the window to let in some fresh air during their sleep and to be able to hear if anyone approached. The distinctive sweet and sticky smell of the corn leaves infiltrated his nostrils. Pungent though it was, at least the height of the stalks would provide an extra level of protection for their hiding place. Far better than the fields of soybeans, which were so prevalent across the Indiana countryside.

Samantha wrinkled her nose, her freckles scrunching into a bunch. "Borrowing a car is a big favor to ask, especially when, at the rate we're going, it'll most likely get damaged or left behind. The only people I can think of are my mom and sister, but they're out of town. Plus, they drove the car to Florida for a church conference. I could call them, but what could they do? It would take a day and a half to drive home. If they flew, then we wouldn't have the car. And despite what most people think of lawyers, my sister and I aren't wealthy with excess funds to be able to go buy another car. The damage to my little Honda is already going to put a major dent in my savings." She puffed out her breath, a little circle of fog forming on her window in the nighttime humidity. "I don't want to cause trouble for either of them."

Reid couldn't fault her for that. He had heard people talk about how they could call on their families for anything, in any kind of distress or trouble. But he'd never experienced that, so how could he presume that she had? If she said she wouldn't, or couldn't, bother her mother and sister, then he would take her word for it.

"That's fine. We'll figure something out." But he couldn't help scrunching his eyebrows together with the perplexity of the situation. "Let's get comfortable and get some sleep."

"Comfortable? In a car?" Maybe Reid had had the kind of college experience where guys sleep in their cars to wait in line for concert tickets. But the most sleeping in a car she had ever done was on a long drive to vacation in Gatlinburg. "Does the seat recline?"

She swiveled around. Lily had taken the entire backseat and she was still curled up in the fetal position. The cargo space was small to begin with, but it was filled. A worn suitcase, a couple of plastic storage totes and three cardboard boxes labeled Books had been crammed in. Probably stuff he thought he would need in the short-term, and he could drive back to wherever he came from for the rest of his possessions. Even with her brain, which couldn't judge the size of anything by her eyeballing it, she could tell she wouldn't fit. And if she lay on top of the containers, she would be at the height of the windows, easy pickings for the thugs. She turned back to the front and felt alongside the seat for the controls or a lever. The lower she could get, the better.

Reid unbuckled his seat belt and turned until he had a knee in the driver's seat. "It's a good thing, I guess, that I haven't found an apartment yet. I have all my worldly belongings in the back, including a pillow and a couple of blankets."

Samantha stifled a gasp. That was everything in the world that he owned? That mattered to him? Of course she couldn't see what was in the tubs, but her possessions would have filled a small moving truck at the very least. What about photo albums or scrapbooks that contained a record of pleasantness in the past? What about souvenirs from family vacations? What about furniture? A bed? A comfortable chair for reading? She turned back to the front to keep an eye out for bad guys, even though it was so dark she wouldn't be able to see anyone until they stood nearly right next to her window. She wouldn't pry into what his worldly belongings consisted of.

A plastic lid flapped behind her as Reid rummaged around in his containers. A moment later, a pillow pushed against the back of her head, shoving her hair into her face. She grabbed the pillow and turned around in her seat just in time to come face-to-face with Reid. She stared for a moment. A streak of lightning flashed, allowing her to see that his blue eyes were flecked with darker hues. He was too close, his masculine stubbly cheek too close, for comfort. Or maybe there was too much comfort in his closeness. Whatever it was, she didn't have the time or desire to analyze it. Her focus was, and always would be, on providing a safe haven for Lily and the adopted children of her clients. That was the final verdict.

She pulled back against the passenger door, allowing him to turn and sit back in the driver's seat. His husky voice wrapped around her like the comforter he held. "Let Lily have the pillow."

"Agreed." Now it was Samantha's turn to lean over into the backseat where Lily snored softly, her head lolling against the headrest. Samantha unfastened Lily's seat belt and lay her down on the seat. As she tucked Reid's pillow underneath Lily's head, Lily only mumbled something incoherent and complied with Samantha's arrangement. Lily's soft snoring resumed, and Samantha turned back to the front, satisfied that the girl would get some rest.

Reid held the edge of a comforter out to her. She grasped it and pulled it over her legs. "It's all I have, so we'll have to share. As the temperature drops, I don't think it'll be too heavy."

"It'll be fine."

Another streak of lightning jagged through the sky. A breath later, torrential rain poured down in sheets. Samantha clutched the edge of the blanket as Reid rolled up the windows. The heavy drops pummeled the Jeep, and Samantha found herself scooting as close as possible to the console that divided her from Reid. She glanced at him, and in another lightning flash, he offered a wobbly smile. She appreciated the effort at consolation, but he didn't look too sure of himself.

"Summer storms don't usually last long." He peered out the window into the inky blackness as if he could see the clouds clearing already. "And this gully washer is actually a good thing. It'll muddy up and perhaps even wash away our tracks down that dirt road. You know, just in case those guys in the SUV are tracking us."

"That makes sense." She prayed Reid was right, because every time she glanced outside the Jeep, she didn't see cornstalks. She saw angry men marching toward her with arms stretched out to grab her and Lily. The door was locked, but the window wouldn't stop a bullet. She was sure of that.

Then, as quickly as it had begun, the downpour lessened to a gentle patter on the roof of the vehicle. Reid leaned toward her. "You okay?"

"Better now that the storm seems to have passed."

"I think we'll be fine here through the night." He paused, holding his breath as if afraid to say what was on his mind.

"What else do you want to say? Considering our circumstances, you might as well spit it out."

"I was wondering about your father. From what I read of him, he's got plenty of money and would, most likely, have an extra car we could use. Maybe we could even hide out at his place while we work with the police some more."

Her father? Now it was Samantha's turn to hold her breath. But hadn't she just told him to tell all? She exhaled softly. "I pray every day for my father's salvation. He desperately needs God in his life. But it hurts too much to have any kind of regular contact with him. In fact, I haven't spoken with him in over a year."

"Right." Reid slid a hand under the comforter to grasp hers and pull it onto the console between them. The warmth of his hold encouraged her to continue.

"When my sister and I were in high school, my father decided he didn't want to be burdened by a family anymore. I was actually the one who found evidence of his unfaithfulness when he returned from a conference. He moved out the next weekend. And what do you think the outcome was when the city's leading divorce attorney with all his knowledge and connections and power decided to divorce his wife?"

"I can imagine."

"But can you imagine the pain, the emotional hurt, that was inflicted on my family? My mother was left destitute, with just barely enough money in alimony to get through a little bit of school. She had always been a mom for us, and even though she was a wonderful mom, those skills don't translate well into the workplace. And he didn't just reject his wife, he rejected us, his children. Me and Mallory."

"I've read about his law practice in *Indianapolis Magazine*. Sounds as if the guy has some of the most prestigious clients in the city. Is that what drove you to law school?"

"I guess, in a backward sort of way, my father determined my career choice. Mallory and I were determined to use the law to try to counter the harm he was doing. We reasoned that the more families we brought together through adoption, perhaps the less damage he was doing by living the high life with money earned from other children's pain. Maybe that doesn't make a lot of sense, but it helped us begin to heal." She clutched her shirt, a familiar ache rising in her sternum. "I don't think we'll ever be completely healed, though."

He rubbed his thumb over the back of her hand, drawing her attention back to the touch. Electricity jolted between them, and she pulled her hand away. She leaned against her window, clutching her hands together, squeezing away the sensation of his touch. Their connection scared her. She had promised herself long ago that she would devote herself to her work.

"What is it?"

"I appreciate your help, but…" Why not just tell him everything? Get it out in the open and then they'd be clear. She released a sigh. "Dad's leaving was one of the most horrible times in my life. Mal and I graduated high school the following year, and everything was still so fresh. We started college, and I was just angry. Angry that my family was torn apart. Angry that my father had ditched us like that. So when this really cute guy with a leather jacket roared in on a motorcycle, I fell for him. Hard. It wasn't long, and we were together all the time, and the pain lessened. When I look back, I can see that there were lots of things that should have warned me about him, but I ignored them. I just wanted someone to want to be with me."

Reid shifted in his seat but didn't take his eyes off her.

"After a few months, we had this big date planned. It sure seemed like a perfect proposal time to me. We were a bit young, but when you're young you don't realize how young you are. You know what I mean?"

He nodded, as if afraid his voice would stop her story.

"So we went out, had a nice supper, all that rigmarole. He brought me back to my apartment, and I thought that was the big moment. I was stupid and blurted it out. *I love you.* But you know what he said? Nothing. He just shook his head and walked away. He dumped me. The end." She crossed her arms across her front to ward off a sudden chill. "I never told anyone, not even my twin. So that's it. Two hurts too many. I appreciate your help, but when this is over and we're back to normal, it's goodbye."

An awkward silence consumed the space between them. Even after telling that story, she wiggled her fingers, a tiny part of her missing his touch. She sneaked a glance at him. A weary, almost sad expression rested on his face as he stared at the steering wheel.

He cleared his throat quietly. "I understand hurt, and I understand not trusting. I wasn't trying to imply anything, just be comforting. But you can rest assured that there's nothing else." He turned to gaze briefly into her eyes, his own burdened with grief and longing. "You wouldn't want to be with me anyway. Too much risk." He turned his back to her as much as the seat would allow and pulled the comforter up to his shoulders.

Risk? Did that mean what she thought it did, that he was just like that guy in college? If so, the sooner the police could catch these men, then the sooner she and Lily could get back to life as normal, and the sooner she could distance herself from Reid Palmer.

And despite the artificial coziness of a late night with an attractive man in a gentle rain, she couldn't allow herself to be taken in by a handsome face again. She reclined her seat as much as possible while still giving Lily enough wiggle room, grateful for the refreshing breeze sneaking in through a crack in the window to cool her warm cheeks.

Reid's whisper filtered through the darkness between them. "One request, if you don't mind. Let's pray about what to do tomorrow regarding those roughnecks. Maybe God will present an answer in the morning."

Samantha pulled the comforter up around her shoulders and nestled her head against the firm headrest. Pray? Since when had Reid Palmer become a praying man? He did seem different than when she had known him before. Was it possible he had truly changed? She closed her eyes, but there wouldn't be much sleep for her tonight with all the questions swirling around in her mind and the lingering comfort from his touch on her hand.

EIGHT

Sharp sunlight pierced through Reid's eyelids. He raised his hand to shield himself even before he opened his eyes. He tried to roll over, and his hind end hit an unyielding barrier. Where was he? He slowly opened his eyes and took in the interior of his Jeep Cherokee. He slapped the visor down, but it only blocked a little of the glare. A gentle snoring reached his ears, and he turned to see a beautiful woman with strawberry blond hair falling across her freckled cheek in his passenger seat. An adorable ten-year-old nose whistled in his backseat.

He bolted upright and hit his head on the ceiling of the SUV. As he rubbed the sore spot, his memory returned like a choke hold. Samantha Callahan. Her ward, Lily. The would-be kidnappers. And he still didn't have a job or a place to live. He opened his eyes a little more. Felt the gentle summer-morning breeze on his forehead as it drifted in through the crack in the window. Sniffed the fresh country air. He wrinkled his nose—cows must be nearby, but it was still a far better awakening than the morning he'd woken up in a jail cell. He hadn't told Samantha any of his story, but what would be the point? Statistics proved that any romantic relationship was a bad idea for both him and whomever he might be involved with. Numbers didn't lie. And she had made it abundantly clear that she was unavailable and would be for...well, ever. Still, she had trusted him with her hurts, and he would honor that by keeping her secrets.

He stepped out of the Jeep and immediately sunk his shoes into an inch of mud. That would muck up the Jeep, but it couldn't be helped now. He stretched his legs, then closed the door softly and watched to see that neither Samantha nor Lily stirred with the sound.

The perimeter of the Jeep was undisturbed—no footprints in the mud, no cornstalks flattened. That was as he expected, since Samantha and Lily were still slumbering in the vehicle. He walked down the now muddy road a ways, filling his lungs with fresh air and his spirit with fresh hope. Despite the trauma of his childhood, his mother had been right—hope always did come in the morning. It was just too bad that it didn't last through the day. But now he was an adult, forging a new way with the help of a trust in the living God, one who could and would direct his paths. He squatted down in the mud and bowed his head, thanking the Lord for their safety through the night and praying for a new course this morning. A course that would lead him to God's will.

Satisfied that their location remained undetected, Reid turned back toward the Jeep. Samantha had emerged and was stepping lightly toward him, the morning sunlight filtering around her. The statistics fled his mind as she approached, and he gave in to the urge to tuck some stray hair behind her ear. She turned toward his hand and held it against her cheek, closing her eyes in the sunshine, apparently savoring their moment alone.

He didn't dare speak. Words didn't seem needful or wanted. Instead, he prayed the Lord would use that touch to fill her with hope for another day.

The moment was over with a cough from the Jeep's backseat. Samantha pulled away, and Reid saw Lily sit up in the backseat, her bedhead fluffed like an '80s hairstyle.

"Good morning." He opened the door and sat down on the seat sideways, scraping as much mud as he could off his shoes on the edge of the running board. "Sleep well?"

"Yep." Lily arched her back to stretch the sleep out. "I slept great. Maybe we should sleep in the car more often, Sam."

Samantha met his gaze and rolled her eyes toward Lily, a slight smile curling her pink lips. Against his wishes, Reid's heart flopped. Did her playful look mean that all was well, even after her rather terse instructions the night before to stay away?

"There is no way we're sleeping in the car ever again, apart from another emergency. You know that." Samantha folded up the comforter as best she could in the confined space. "Any chance we could get some breakfast?" she asked Reid.

"Yeah, I'm hungry," Lily said.

Reid pulled his door shut as he slid all the way into his seat. "I haven't seen any prints in the mud, so I think we're good to go eat."

"Are we going to have to drive-through again or can we get out? Maybe use the facilities?" Samantha asked.

"If we don't pick up a tail, I think we'll be okay getting out. I'll drive to the next suburb for safety since they're looking for you in Heartwood Hill." He started the engine and threw it into Drive. The Jeep slogged through the mud and finally emerged onto the main, paved road.

Lily bounced around in the backseat. "Can we go to that place where they have the blackberries in the pancakes and the syrup in cute little jars?"

"Sounds good to me, but I need a strong cup of coffee."

He glanced in the rearview mirror just in time to see her screw up her face in an expression of disgust. "Yuck."

"How about milk? Good for a growing girl." He glanced at Samantha to find her watching him, a smirk forming, but he couldn't tell if it was upset at his friendliness with her ward or appreciation that he could talk to a child. Either way, it didn't matter. He wasn't going to put himself in a position where he could hurt another person, especially someone he was beginning to care about.

A few miles down the road, his phone rang. "Yeah?"

"Got a minute?" Derek's confident tone sounded in his ear, bolstering Reid's own confidence that his police training had not been in vain if he could continue to protect Samantha and Lily.

Reid chuckled. "Got nothing but time."

"Okay, so we got Samantha's Honda towed

to a body shop. She'll have to deal with it from there, but we couldn't get any prints. I'm guessing he never touched it. She wasn't in it, so he didn't need to."

"Right. I don't think getting the car fixed is a high priority right now, but text me the number for the place, and I'll pass it on."

"Good enough. We also ran the prints we lifted from her house last night. Nothing except the residents'. The guy probably wore gloves."

"Figures." Reid intercepted a quizzical glance from Samantha, and he shook his head. *In a minute*, he mouthed.

"You also mentioned the gas station, but since he went in to prepay, I'm assuming it was in cash. A card would have been swiped at the pump."

"That's what I thought, too. No help there. What about the hotel? How did he figure out what room we were in? Did he pay off the clerk?"

"No. The night clerk was out back on the phone with his girlfriend. The perp probably stepped behind the desk and searched through the computer. Those programs can't be that hard to figure out. Point and click." Irritation tinged Derek's voice.

"I registered in my name, though. He wouldn't know my name."

"He could have just looked for the most recent check-in. Maybe he saw you pull up and thought the dark of the hotel room would be good cover. He could have been sitting in the parking lot, biding his time until the clerk left."

A groan escaped Reid. "So now they know who I am, as well?"

"Probably so."

Reid rubbed his forehead. This wasn't helping the situation. "Okay, what about the guy I knocked out at the superstore?"

"Dead end there, too, bub. Store employees never found anyone out of place, let alone a guy lying unconscious in a remote part of the back area."

"What?" In the passenger seat, Samantha startled at his loud tone. She glared at him and tucked her hair behind her ear. He'd better keep it down. Panic wouldn't help. "No one? He disappeared?"

"Yeah, gone. And I checked at the hospital. No one appeared at the ER last night."

Frustration bubbled up like heartburn. He had had visual contact with this guy, but with his sunglasses and cap, he knew it wouldn't help to work with a sketch artist. As best Reid could tell, no one else had seen him anyway, except maybe the cashier at the gas station. But that place had been so busy that the cashier had probably never even looked up from the register. "All right. Then, I'll see what I can find out about the father. Maybe that's the connection?"

"You never know. But these guys are good, maybe professionals, so watch yourself."

"Definitely. But we're professionals, too." What had he said? Reid gulped air, wishing he could jump in a time machine and undo what he had just said. How could he still think of himself as a professional law enforcement officer after the way he had disgraced his shield? The shield he no longer carried. Old trains of thought were proving harder to leave behind than he had anticipated.

"Hey, man?" Derek's voice brought him out of his reverie.

"Yeah?"

"Glad to have you back."

Sure. One person was glad to have him back. He had a long way to go before his other relationships were restored and Heartwood Hill could be called home.

The privacy of the bathroom was a welcome relief from the close quarters shared with Reid all night. Samantha rubbed lotion slowly into her hands, savoring the vanilla scent, the feeling of femininity and the smidgen of normalcy it contained. If she couldn't be at home enjoying her regular routine, this was the next best thing.

The drive to a neighboring suburb had consumed a half hour full of checking about for black SUVs, but none had been spotted. When they'd arrived at the restaurant, Reid had parked behind an adjacent building to hide the Jeep.

Now he stood guard outside the door. When they emerged, he darted his gaze around the lobby crammed with candles and decorations for sale, probably looking for a thug lurking behind the collection of ceramic roosters. He ushered them to the hostess station, where he asked for a booth in the back. He leaned into Samantha with a low tone. "It might hide us a little better. Just in case."

She raised an eyebrow at him as they wove between the tables filled with customers sipping hot brew, salting scrambled eggs and cutting up French toast. A nervous laugh threatened in her throat. She was almost in disbelief that just yesterday she was looking forward to a fun summer weekend with Lily.

He hunched and peered at her with a suspicious look, then straightened and smiled as if he was trying to lighten the mood. "Bad guys have to eat, too, so you never know where they'll show up."

"That's true, Sam." Lily fist-bumped Reid.

Samantha pinched her lips at him and took her seat. His levity fell short, his comment only serving to remind her that those bad guys really could be lurking anywhere. That sneaky, nervous laugh choked her, and she sputtered, grabbing for a glass of water.

They quickly ordered pancakes, and Reid filled her in on his conversation with Derek. She breathed a sigh of relief that Reid's former police buddy was helping them, but they were still left without any answers or any idea about how to move forward.

She looked around the restaurant in what felt like a ridiculous attempt to see if anyone looked suspicious. She wasn't trained in surveillance and had no idea what to do except hide. A slurp from Reid as he held his water glass to his lips caught her attention, and she slumped her shoulders. Despite his reputation, he had been kind and protective. In fact, she and Lily probably wouldn't be here waiting for blackberry pancakes for breakfast if not for his efforts. There simply was no other recourse but to muddle through under his guard and pray they all came out of it alive.

Quiet sounds drew her attention to Lily sitting on the inside of the booth. The girl was smooshing a honey packet against the table until it threatened to burst.

"Lily, enough, before you spray us all with that sticky stuff." Samantha tried not to let her weariness show in her tone, but her instruction still came out as irritated.

Lily slouched in the booth and returned the packet to its holder. She rummaged around in her pocket and retrieved her spy sunglasses. She quickly put them on and popped her head above the booth. "Look, Sam. I can tell you when our breakfast is coming."

"Hey, Lil. Maybe you'll be a police officer someday. Detective even." Reid's eyebrows shot up like question marks.

A grin spread across Lily's face. "Maybe a secret agent. I could do surveillance."

Samantha rubbed her fingers together under the table, trying not to pick at a fingernail again. At this rate, she would soon be down to nubs. Could she stomach a child working in such a dangerous field? "Lily, you really shouldn't wear sunglasses inside. It's rude."

"I'm just trying them out, and you wouldn't let me squish the honey."

"While we eat, I can give you some pointers on catching bad guys," Reid said. "Give you a head start above the others who apply to the police academy." He smiled at Samantha as if they shared a secret.

Samantha ripped at a fingernail until it tore, the quick pain slicing through her fingertip. What was he doing, getting all chummy with Lily? Sure, they could have polite conversation, but it wasn't in the child's best interests to get attached and form a relationship that would just have to end. She shook her head no at Reid, a sadness of surprising intensity soaking through her, and the smile slipped from his face.

"Here comes our breakfast," Lily announced.

Reid leaned out of the booth and gazed past Samantha. "Thanks, kiddo."

A moment later, the waitress was placing steaming plates of pancakes and eggs and bacon in front of them. The aroma of breakfast meat assaulted her, and her stomach growled in impatience.

Reid thanked the server, and before she could pick up her fork, he bowed his head. "God, we thank You for this breakfast and for the security of this booth. Keep Your guiding hand on us and show us to safety. Amen."

It was over before Samantha could even lay down her fork. She sat there stunned, staring at the stubble on Reid's chin, unable and unwilling to make eye contact. His fork scraped his plate, and she shook her head to clear her thoughts.

It didn't take long for the ten-year-old next to her and the grown man across from her to finish their breakfasts. Reid sat with a second cup of coffee while Samantha finished her hotcakes. The waitress left the bill so exactly between the two of them that it looked as if she had used a ruler to measure the distance.

He sipped and returned the cup to the table with a thunk. "I'm a little concerned about our cash supply. To keep on the move and undetected, we ought not use credit. Either of us. But quite frankly, my wallet doesn't have much more in it." He shrugged, seemingly nonchalant about his admission of a lack of funds.

But money hadn't even occurred to her. She chewed slowly, buying some time as she recounted the events and the expenses of the past eighteen or so hours. Not once had she offered to pay for anything. In her defense, she had been a bit preoccupied with keeping both Lily and herself safe. But now they had Reid for protection, and the police were involved. She needed to pony up some dough.

"There's a branch of my bank just down the street. Since I'm the reason for all the trouble, what if I stop by the ATM and withdraw some money? I'm not exactly Miss Moneybags, but hopefully all this will be over soon anyway. Would that be all right if I access my bank account?"

"Sounds fine. It's not as if we'll be leaving a digital trail of our whereabouts."

Reid paid the bill, and they returned to the Jeep. A comfortable and secure feeling washed over Samantha as she slid into the passenger seat. But then, spending a lot of time in one particular place could engender a sense of belonging. She fastened her seat belt as she wondered how many more miles she would ride in that seat.

A couple of blocks down the main drag, Reid steered the Jeep into the drive-through lane. As he approached the machine, he reached over to her. "Got your card?"

She dug it out of her billfold and handed it over. He slid it into the reader, then turned to her when the machine prompted him for the security code. "What's your PIN?"

"PIN?" She hadn't anticipated having to give him such personal information. She should have driven or just gone into the bank.

"Yeah. Personal identification number."

"I know what it stands for." Still she sat, unable to speak it out loud.

Reid pleated his lips at her. "I'm not going to

do anything with it. I couldn't anyway without your card, and you can always change it later."

He had a point. She stated the number slowly, in a half whisper, watching as he punched in each digit.

A moment later, the screen went blank. No card and no cash were ejected. Then the welcome image returned, as if they had never attempted a transaction.

"Where's my card?"

Reid tapped the screen and pushed the clear button a couple of times.

Nothing.

"What's going on?" Panic clutched at her insides, twisting her lungs into a knot. If the machine ate her card, didn't that mean something was terribly wrong?

"I don't know. Let's go inside and find out." He drove around to the front and parked. "With all the security and cameras, we'll be fine."

An armed guard stood at the entrance. Maybe they could just set up camp in the vault?

Samantha approached the closest teller just as a woman in a trim navy blue suit with the bank logo emblazoned on the jacket pocket rounded the corner. The teller offered a practiced grin. "Good morning. How can I help you?"

Samantha wanted to collapse on the counter

and finally let the tears she had been holding go, but instead she glanced around to see who was listening. "I was just at the ATM, and it kept my card. I'd like to withdraw some cash."

The woman in the suit stepped forward, and the teller withdrew, her gaze on the floor. "Samantha Callahan?"

"Yes?" She looked like a manager, but why would she know Samantha?

"Let's have a seat in my office."

She led them to a cubicle and gestured to two chairs, pulling in a third for Lily. Behind the desk, she unbuttoned her blazer and sat, leaning her elbows on the counter. "The ATM kept your card because our computer shows a hold on your account."

NINE

Dizziness threatened to overtake Samantha, and she stared at the ceiling until it passed. "What do you mean, a hold? I have a checking and a savings, with nearly three thousand dollars combined, and I need to withdraw some of my money." She cast a glance at Reid. No money meant no food, no shelter, no gas.

"The system will not allow me to access your accounts, and the ATM is programmed to keep the card of anyone suspicious."

"I'm suspicious? I'm a loyal customer."

"Of course." Her patronizing smile burned in Samantha's chest. "But we don't keep any paper records, so I only know what the computer shows me."

Reid leaned forward, a deep crease across his brow. "Who authorized the hold?" He glanced toward Samantha, and she nodded her appreciation to him.

"I don't know who placed the hold, sir. All

I can see on my monitor is that it came from the highest level."

"And what happens now? Why would a hold be placed on the accounts?"

The manager picked up her phone. "No reason is given here, sir. I can call our technical department and see what they can find out."

"Yes, please."

As the woman dialed and then transferred her attention to that conversation, Samantha turned to Reid. His brow remained furrowed as he stared at the carpet. "What's going on here? Does this have anything to do with the guys who want to kidnap us?"

He slowly veered his attention to her, as if she was pulling him out of deep thought. "Probably. And that means that they are much more sophisticated than I thought."

"But what would be the purpose of this?"

"To get your attention. To limit your options for running and hiding. To draw you out. To make you suffer."

"Okay. Enough." She cast a glance back at Lily, who was drawing on a piece of copier paper. "I get it. Can we keep it quiet?"

"I think we'll find answers faster if we involve her. She's got a great mind, and she might know something that you don't, especially if this has to do with her past. And you might be the key to drawing it out, since you've been her friend and guardian all this time." He glanced at the bank manager, who was still deep in her phone conversation. "I'm almost sure now that those thugs are hired or on the take. Whoever they're working for probably cleared your account." He turned to Lily. "Hey, kiddo. Can I ask you some questions?"

Lily looked up from her paper. "Yeah."

"You said your father was an accountant."

"Something like that. I know he worked with a bunch of boring numbers on the computer."

"What company did he work for?"

Lily looked quizzically at Samantha. "I can answer that," Samantha said. "It was the local pharmaceutical company, Zigfried Pharmaceuticals."

"Did he have any difficult coworkers? Did he ever mention any run-ins with anyone at work?"

"I don't know."

Samantha licked her lips. Maybe she could ask the same question in a way Lily would understand. "When you were living with him, did your father ever act strange or different after he came home from work? Or did he work long hours? You know, come home really late for supper?"

Lily shrugged. "Yeah, all the time. But that was how it was after Mom died. Dad was just so sad all the time. I figured he didn't miss her as much if he stayed at work."

Samantha pressed her fist to her aching heart. She renewed her vow to make as normal a home as possible for Lily. No child should have to endure the loss of both parents.

Reid shifted in his chair to turn toward Lily a little more. "Did you ever see anything on his computer?"

"Just numbers."

Samantha glanced at the manager. She was still on the phone but made eye contact and offered a plastic smile. Samantha leaned into Reid and kept her voice down. "The girl is ten. How is she going to know what she's looking at?"

"Fine. Objection sustained." With a slight smile, he aimed the next question back to Lily. "Ever overhear any conversations? Anything suspicious?"

"Nope." Lily held up her paper. "But look at the cool robot I'm drawing. What do you think?"

The bank manager cleared her throat as she crashed the telephone receiver back in the cradle. Samantha flinched at the attempt to get their attention.

"So." The woman steepled her fingers with a somber expression. "I've talked with tech support. To some extent, their hands are tied because of the high level of approval on this. But after I explained the confusion, they said they'll get their security guys going on the problem. If you'd like to leave me your phone number, I'll keep you informed."

"That's it? We can't get this figured out today?"

"Something like this takes time, ma'am. We're doing everything we can."

Reid touched her arm, a gesture she took to be reassurance that all would eventually be well. Being comforted was nice, but since there was no knowledge of the future, anxiety threatened to consume her.

"Samantha's phone is broken. Can you call my number?"

"Of course, sir."

With nothing else to accomplish at the bank, handshakes were offered and Samantha found herself in the Jeep. Again. She stared at the corner of the bank building, where a surveillance camera hovered, recording all who came and went. Surveillance sounded like a good idea, but if the camera never recorded anything helpful, what was the point? She suppressed what seemed like the thousandth sigh that had wanted to bubble up since yesterday afternoon and listened in on Reid's phone call to Derek, his officer friend.

"No, no. I understand. It's a small department. Any chance of some help from the Indianapolis PD?"

Lily spoke up from the backseat, but Samantha shushed her. If her life and the life of her ward were at risk, she wanted to know all the details.

"Okay. Well, let me know, good or bad. Thanks." Reid touched the screen and put the phone in his pocket. "Derek can't promise anything because their resources are limited when it comes to finding computer hackers. It's a small town with a small police department."

"That makes sense." But nothing else made sense. What did those thugs want from them? If she knew, she would hand it over and end the whole ordeal. Get back to normal life. "I have no idea what to do next. But can we figure this out? Who are these guys and what do they want?"

"We can't keep driving around. You know the area better than I do. Is there a park with some privacy nearby? Someplace to get out and stretch our legs while staying hidden?"

"There's a big church on the north side of

town that dug a pond out behind their two-story building. They put in a picnic pavilion, the kind with a fireplace at either end, and some walking trails." She sucked in a deep breath. "If I remember correctly, you can't see any of it from the road."

Confusion hazed her mind like the summer humidity. She couldn't pinpoint why, but she wanted, needed even, Reid's approval. She needed it like she needed that first cup of coffee the morning after a late night at work.

"Sounds like a plan. It'll give us a moment to breathe and think. How do I get there?"

Samantha dictated the directions to the church, hoping she was right about the seclusion of the picnic area. She kneaded her palms together and pushed the panic back down to her stomach.

As Reid steered the Jeep, he kept an eye on his female passengers. Samantha was slender and willowy and wouldn't be difficult at all to carry off, if a large man were so inclined. And Lily? The girl was like a stick figure. She had spunk, but spunk couldn't always hold its own against pure muscle. "Considering our circumstances, you know what you two need?"

"A hot shower?"

"A latte?"

"Some instruction on how to defend yourself."

Samantha seemed to sag in her seat, disappointed perhaps, while Lily's face lit with a smile. "You're gonna teach me how to fight?"

"I didn't say fight. I said defend yourself. In case of attack. And I'll do my best in the confines of the car. First, when you fight back, appear strong. Don't cower like a dog with its tail between its legs. Scream if you can. Scream as if you're on fire."

"I can scream real good. Wanna hear?"

"No," Samantha exclaimed, holding her palm up to stop Lily. "Reid knows you can scream. Right, Reid?"

Reid glanced at Lily's crestfallen expression in the rearview mirror. "I'm sure you can scream plenty, kiddo." He offered a grin to Samantha. "You, too."

"Hmm." A watchful maternal look creased Samantha's brow, as if she understood the necessity of self-protection but worried about her child's response to the instruction.

No matter her comfort level, Reid continued, convinced of the appropriateness of the training. "Your elbows and your knees are your strongest hitting points. You have lots of power there. When you hit, aim for the weak spots on a man." He paused. This was foreign territory to him. How to approach delicately? "Do you know where those are?"

Lily giggled, an effervescence that bubbled out of her current state of childhood. It was a pleasant tinkling in his ear that made Reid glad he had dared to ask.

Samantha pinched her lips. "She does. We've had similar talks before."

"Good." Why was he surprised? Samantha was proving herself to be a capable and caring mother.

Samantha cocked her head at him. "Why are you being so helpful? Giving so much instruction to a girl?" She hesitated, as if uncertain whether to continue her line of questioning. "The old Reid I knew in law school would have turned on those bad guys, guns loaded, and let them have it, just to be able to use the weapon. But now you seem so…protective. Paternal, almost."

He wanted to stop the Jeep and explain everything. He wanted to tell her about his glorious conversion and his ongoing struggle to leave his past there, in the past. He wanted to grab her hand and explain his incomprehensible feelings for her, his need for her to see him as a new and improved man, his desire for a normal family life that could never be fulfilled.

Instead, he shrugged and affected what he figured was a look of nonchalance. "They're after me as well now."

But as he held up his elbow to demonstrate to Lily in the backseat the strength of that point of the body, his forearm brushed against the sleeve of Samantha's shirt. Like a sponge soaking up water, he absorbed the softness of the touch, the closeness to her in the enclosed Jeep, the scent of her strawberry shampoo. He exhaled, pushing out all thoughts of the future save for the one image he knew would be the truth. Him. Alone. There was no other way.

"So, kiddo, the elbow. Keep it controlled. Wild movements don't have strength." If only he'd known the virtues of keeping control in his earlier days. What would his life be now if he hadn't succumbed to his own wild movements? He tamped down a sigh and focused on the feisty ten-year-old in his backseat, praying that the woman in the front was listening, as well. "If you're attacked from the front, aim for the attacker's nose. Yell as you hit. It'll add strength. I know it sounds weird, but it's true."

Lily thrust her elbow into the back of the seat. "Is that why those tennis players on TV grunt so loud when they hit the ball?"

Samantha chuckled. "Probably so." She

pointed out the windshield and looked at Reid. "Turn right at that next light."

"Okay, so grunt and hit. What else?"

"If you're attacked from the back, slam your elbow into your attacker's gut. Or, even better, aim at his face, although you might be a little short still for that."

"Not for long." Lily held up both arms to flex her biceps.

"The face is delicate, especially the eyes, and that'll stop him for a minute or more. If he wraps his arm around you to hold you still, step forward and then to the side, like the two-step." He tossed a smile in Samantha's direction. "That can throw the attacker off balance just enough for you, either of you, to wiggle free and run away."

The seat trembled as if Lily were moving her feet against it in the back. "So step forward and then to the side."

"You got it. And I have no doubt that you, kiddo, would be able to outrun any adult, since you're so lightweight and energetic."

"What about Sam? Would she be able to get away?"

Reid swallowed, pushing away the painful image of a villainous man with his hands on Samantha. He turned to see her watching him with large, luminous eyes. "Yes. Since you're so…so lithe, you should be able to out-run just about any adult male as well, at least far enough to get to where there are other people." Heat crawled up his neck, and he rubbed a hand against his nape. Had he said too much about her appearance, especially after her comments the night before? He didn't want her to get the wrong idea, but he wasn't sure what the wrong idea and what the right idea were anymore.

"Hey, you want to see something cool I learned to do with a phone? Can I see yours, Mr. Palmer?" Lily apparently had had enough self-defense training. Perhaps a distraction was best anyway.

"Turn left on Maple up there, and you'll see it." Samantha glanced in the side mirror. "I haven't seen anyone following. You?"

Reid shook his head and complied with her instructions to turn as he handed his phone to Lily. She leaned through the seats as much as her seat belt would allow. "My friend Abby showed me how." She flicked her finger up on the main screen and then tapped an icon. Reid looked away from the road for a brief moment to see that the icon looked like a flashlight. "See? Like this."

A flash of light nearly as strong as the lightning last night blinded him temporarily. Spots danced in his vision as Samantha shielded her eyes. "Come on, Lil. Put that away. I don't need to know anything like that."

Lily tapped again, and the same flash appeared. "You can leave the light on if you want, but I think just the flash is fun."

"It's not fun. It's dangerous, especially with Reid trying to drive. If you flashed that in darker circumstances, we wouldn't be able to see a thing for several seconds."

"Aw, seriously, Sam? You don't like it?"

Samantha clucked her tongue. "Seriously, young lady. Give it back to Mr. Palmer."

Reid rubbed his eye as the color spots stopped twirling. "If she calls you young lady, kiddo, you better obey."

Lily flopped against the seat. "Yeah, figured that one out a while back." She held the phone out to Reid.

Reid turned into the parking lot of a two-story structure with a cross outlined in the brick. "Is this it? It looks like a mall."

"This is it. Follow that one-lane driveway around back."

A white privacy fence surrounded what looked like a day care playground with a slide and swing set rising above the barrier. "The parking lot is empty, and I haven't seen a tail of any kind." He pulled around the building and spotted the pavilion and the pond, as well as a smaller playground nearby.

He stepped out of the Jeep and slammed the door behind him as Samantha and Lily joined him from the passenger side. A quick scan of the area revealed a quiet country setting, probably completely unknown to all but the members of the church.

Samantha stopped at the edge of the parking lot and inhaled deeply. "Maybe, just for a moment, I can pretend that none of this has happened."

"Okay, but only for that moment." Reid stopped beside her, waiting for her to move forward. "Maybe we should practice those defensive moves. Just in case."

"Do we have to?" Lily backed toward the pond, her head tilted sideways. "Hear those frogs in the pond? Think I could catch one?"

Samantha shook her head and grinned. "Go ahead, but don't fall in. The last thing I need right now is a bunch of muddy clothes." Lily skipped to the water's edge, less than a stone's throw from the pavilion. Samantha turned to Reid. "Do you think that's all right?"

"I think so. It's close." He touched the small of her back to guide her into the pavilion. "Let's sit at that picnic table closest to the pond and see what we can piece together."

"Well, you said at the bank that you think those guys are hired. That would mean there is someone else behind this."

"Yes. Someone with some computer savvy."

"Is that why you keep asking about Lily's father and what he did on computers?"

"Exactly." Reid ran a hand through his hair. "Remember the scrapbook? Lily's mementos of her father? It was the most torn-up thing in your entire house."

"So they're looking for something? Something they think we have?"

"Or some knowledge you possess."

"That's the most confusing part. I don't know anything. I barely knew the man." She ran a finger over her lips, deep in thought.

"Maybe you know something you don't know you know."

"Well, that clears it right up." She grinned, a sparkle in her eye.

Reid allowed himself to grin back. Gratitude for her levity filled him. Perhaps this moment to breathe would be beneficial to them all, but he couldn't let them linger. Movement seemed to be the best way to avoid detection. "At the hotel, you said that Lily's father gave her a key chain. Where is it?"

"It's in my bag, in your Jeep. Want me to get it?"

He held out his palm "No, you stay put. I'll just bring the whole bag." He jogged back to the vehicle, unwilling to allow her to leave the security of the pavilion. A moment later, he laid it on the table next to her.

She dug around and extracted a set of keys with a silver heart-shaped key chain the size of a fifty-cent piece. "Lily wanted it to stay safe, so I put it on my regular key chain. We knew neither of us would lose it that way."

Reid removed the heart from the other chain and held it in the palm of his hand. One half was plain silver. The other half was covered in crystals. Rhinestones, maybe, or bling, he thought he'd heard it called. Whatever it was, there was a clear dividing line down the middle of the heart.

He tried to wedge a fingernail in the division, but his nails were trimmed too short.

"Look here." He pointed to the line as Samantha leaned in close. The scent of strawberries and wildflowers made his head swim, and he swallowed hard. "I think the heart comes apart. Can you work on it?"

She held the heart in her fingers and pried at it. It popped open, revealing the end of a computer flash drive. "I had no idea. I thought it was just a pretty bauble. A thoughtful gift from a father to his daughter."

Reid just stared. "It was thoughtful. Quite a bit more thoughtful than you thought." He shook his head. Had another piece of the puzzle been found, and if so, what did it mean? What was on the flash drive, and why was it so important? Was this what the thugs were after? "We need to see what's on it, but I don't have a laptop. My old one crashed, and I was going to buy a new one after I got to town."

"What about my office?"

"No. They're probably keeping tabs on the place."

"The public library?"

Could they sneak in? Remain undetected? What were the chances of being found out? Reid sighed. "Best not. It's the *public* library."

Samantha snapped the heart back together and handed it to Reid as if it was a poisonous spider. Fear was etched across her face. "I don't want it." She glanced toward Lily, who was leaning precariously over the water's edge with her back to them. "Let's find those guys, give them the flash drive and then let me go home with Lily."

"We don't know that that's all they want. And if they'll resort to violence, there's something illegal here. Those guys need to be brought to justice."

Samantha pushed herself up from the table

and walked to the edge of the cement floor of the pavilion. She stared toward Lily for a moment, and then raised her hands to her face as her shoulders began to shake. Her gentle sobbing grabbed at Reid's heart.

What he wanted to do he could never do. He should never even think about doing it.

He wanted to wrap her in his embrace and whisper to her that he hated that she was scared and hurting. That he cared for her. An image flashed in his mind. His own father, kneeling down next to his mother, in that very embrace and whispering those exact words. The father, now an inmate, comforting his mother, the victim.

What good was his faith if, in the end, he would still turn out just like his father? Perhaps, no matter what his efforts to change or his faith in God, he was still condemned. The numbers swam in his vision, the statistics that showed that children of abusers typically grow up to be violent themselves.

He pushed the numbers and accusations from his mind and strode toward Samantha. He wrapped his arms around her slender, shaky shoulders, and she turned into him, letting his T-shirt soak up her tears.

As her sobs quieted, he stroked her silky hair. Lily had moved to the side of the pond and seemed oblivious to them. He could stand there forever, holding her, protecting her. But it couldn't last. He wasn't made for relationships. "We ought to move on," he whispered, and he drew away, coldness seeping between them even in the midst of the humid summer day.

TEN

Samantha called to Lily that it was time to go. Go where, she wasn't sure, but she shouldered her bag as she watched Lily toss her stick into the middle of the pond in a long, graceful arc and trudge toward the Jeep.

The church quickly disappeared from the Jeep's side mirror as rows of townhomes whizzed by in the afternoon sunshine, morphing into single-family homes and then back to the commercial strip of Heartwood Hill. She swallowed down the bile that threatened in her throat. The thugs hadn't found them yet, but wasn't it inevitable? Would they be able to escape again?

She closed her eyes and fought back more tears.

A gentle hand touched her shoulder. "Sam? Are you okay?"

A verse came unbidden. *She girds herself*

with strength, and strengthens her arms. She needed to be strong for Lily. "I'll be fine."

Reid reached over to squeeze her hand, then returned both to the wheel. "We seem to be catching a break. I haven't seen anything as we've been driving. But we better stay off my phone," he said quietly. "Just in case they're tracking us."

"You think they found us through your phone?"

"Could be. They discovered my identity at the hotel last night, so maybe they're tracking me now. We may never find out, but for now, I think we better not use my phone anymore."

Samantha groaned. When was this going to end? It only seemed to be getting worse. "Perhaps Lily and I would be just as safe at home as with you." What was she saying? He had gone out of his way to take care of them, but fear had snaked its way up her spine.

"Wait a minute." He held out his hands as if to ward her off.

"What if you can't protect us? What if you decide to do whatever it takes to take care of number one? You." Her worries burned in her chest, a whisper of appreciation for Reid flicking through her stress. There had been plenty of opportunities for him to leave them on their own, yet he still sat in the driver's seat. How could she think such a thing, let alone give it voice?

"Now, hold on." Antagonism flickered in his eyes like the sheet lightning they'd seen last night, but it was soon washed away by the rain of his own tears. Clouds of remorse seemed to settle in as he turned to her when he stopped at a red light. "If that's what you think, there's nothing I can say to prove otherwise to you. But you're going to have to go on faith. Faith that God is protecting us. Faith that my goal is to protect you and Lily."

"It'll be fine, Sam." Lily's gentle tone infused calm into the charged atmosphere.

The light turned green, but before he hit the accelerator, Reid turned around to Lily. Samantha saw him mouth *thank you* to the girl.

There was no way the girl could know the end result, but it was sweet of her to say so. Yet that part of Samantha's mind and spirit that had been lied to and hurt before by two different men wanted to nurture the seed of doubt that had been planted. Bad things came in threes, right? So here was Mr. Three. But he had changed, hadn't he? He had proved it over and over. His talk about God and change and prayer wasn't just an act.

Reid pulled into a convenience store and parked next to the side of the building, behind a large cargo van that would hide the Jeep from the road. He swiveled in his seat toward her and grasped her hand, his touch warm and comforting.

"I've said it once, but I'll say it again. As much as you want to hear it. I'm sorry. I'm sorry I was a jerk in law school. I'm sorry you have that memory of me." He paused to swallow. "Will you forgive me?"

Forgiveness? That was where the rubber met the road for a Christian. Samantha rolled her shoulders as if she could shrug off his request. As important as her faith was to her, she wasn't very good at forgiveness. Her relationship with her father was a testament to that sorry fact. But now there were young eyes and ears in the backseat of that Jeep, watching and waiting for her to say the right thing. To set a godly example.

"Y-yes." Remorse burned within her. "I'm sorry I doubted you. Will you forgive me?"

"Definitely."

The late-afternoon sun slanted through the Jeep as Lily clapped her hands. "Good. That's done. Now can we get something to eat?"

Reid offered her a tenuous smile. "It is getting close to suppertime. I was going to run in here and get a burner phone. I think you'll be safe here for a couple of minutes, especially since no one from the road can see us. While I'm gone, think about where we might be able to get another car and some cash. Sound good?"

Lily tipped her head toward Reid. "Good, but add to your list one of those gigantic candy bars for me. Okay?"

"Depends on what Samantha says."

"Fine, but make sure it's chocolate. No nuts." The soothing powers of the cacao bean might provide some temporary relief, but what would happen the next time those thugs showed up? They couldn't keep running indefinitely. He wanted her to say that they could go to her father. That her father would help them and take care of them. Dealing with her father after more than a year of hurt and estrangement? Even that would be better than this continual chase. But would she be able to utter those words when Reid returned?

Reid scanned the parking lot as he approached the store, but nothing suspicious presented itself. It seemed they had escaped again. But the running was becoming wearisome. When would he finally be able to find that apartment, settle in with his take-out Chinese and get started on his new life? Whatever the Lord's plan was in this, he couldn't see it.

And if Samantha didn't agree to call her father... Well, he had no idea what to do next.

A flash of pink caught his eye. He turned to see Samantha and Lily walking toward him and the door. Lily caught up and grabbed his hand. "We're tired of the Jeep. Can't we come in with you?"

"Sure." It might actually be safer if they stayed together. At least, Reid would feel better if the would-be kidnappers' targets were within his line of sight. He grabbed the door and held it open for Samantha. How natural would it feel to hold her hand in his, like Lily had done with him? Would it seem as though they were a regular family? But that wasn't a thought he should entertain.

A dull ached settled into his heart. All he had wanted was to be believed and trusted in the community of Heartwood Hill. But now, would that ever be possible? Perhaps he should give up the dream and leave town as soon as Samantha and Lily were safe.

He led her to the refrigerated section and gestured toward the wide selection of pops and teas. "What's your poison?"

She pursed her lips at him, trying to adopt a pouty look, but she couldn't seem to keep it from morphing into a grin. "Is that really the most tactful way to ask, considering the fact that we're running for our lives?"

So far, the thugs hadn't tried to kill them, but that was a fine point Reid didn't want to bring up. If she was going to smile at him, he would stay quiet and appreciate her beauty, even as it radiated around her red-rimmed eyes. "Sorry." He affected a mock bow and returned her grin. "I apologize again."

She swept past him and selected a raspberry tea. "Is this to go with my candy bar?"

"Definitely."

Lily pulled a can out of the refrigerator. "Unless you want to put it on your puffy eyes. Amanda, my friend at school, said her mother puts cucumbers on her eyes."

"What?" She took off for a revolving display of reading glasses and peered in the tiny mirror at the top. "Are my eyes swollen? From the crying?"

"Not really. But you know Colton from church? He told me his cousin who lives in Ohio got picked on by a bully at school and he came home with a black eye, so his parents went in to talk to the teacher and the other kid's parents, but that only made the other kid more mad at Colton, so he gave him another black eye, and eventually that kid got suspended from school."

"Everyone has a story." She gently touched the pad of her middle finger to the skin around her eye. "Lovely. Maybe I need to pick up some more foundation next time I'm at the drugstore."

"No. You're beautiful just the way God made you." He reached up and twisted a strand of ginger hair around his finger, treasuring the softness and the oddly intimate moment in the middle of the convenience store.

Intimate? What was he thinking? He jerked his gaze up to hers. She watched his gesture, but he couldn't read any expression or thought or emotion on her face. He pulled his hand away and stuffed his fist down in his pocket, turning to select his own can from the refrigerated case.

They chose their candy bars, solid chocolate for Samantha and chocolate with Rice Krispies for Lily. Reid selected a burner phone and a card with minutes and approached the cashier.

The middle-aged woman rang up their purchases but seemed to keep one eye on Samantha. A dozen lapel pins were scattered across her employee vest, her attempt, he supposed, to help spread awareness of breast cancer and literacy programs and domestic violence. Reid pulled out his wallet and selected his last couple of twenties to pay the bill. When she handed Reid his change, he stuffed it in his pocket and turned Samantha and Lily toward the door. In the Jeep, he turned the key in the ignition to get the air-conditioning on but left it in Park. He drummed his fingers on the wheel, uncertain of where to go and what to do next. He didn't have anywhere to take them, and unless they got arrested for something, they couldn't just hang out at the police station. They could try another hotel, but he wasn't eager for another narrow escape, especially with no guarantee of a getaway next time. He glanced out his peripheral vision. Samantha had the visor down and was examining her eyes in the mirror. Did he have to ask her outright if they could call her father?

"Where now, Mr. Palmer?" The sound of tearing paper issued from the backseat, and soon the sound of munching filled the vehicle.

"Well, these guys are good, whoever they are, so there's not much for the police to go on. My friend, Derek, the one you met at your house, is doing all he can. But for right now, we just need to stay low and try to figure out what's going on."

Samantha shifted uncomfortably in her seat and puffed out a quiet exhalation that ruffled her hair. "Let's call my dad."

Finally. Did he dare to utter the words, to give her a possible out? "Are you sure?"

She heaved a sigh across the Jeep. "Yes. He could help, if he's willing. He owns three vehicles, so he ought to be able to spare one. I'm fairly sure he keeps plenty of cash on hand, always ready to impress his latest girlfriend. And he has a computer that, hopefully, he'll let us use to see what's on that flash drive."

Reid hated to push her into a difficult situation with a difficult relationship, but he couldn't see any other way. If the guy had the least bit of feeling for his daughter, he ought to be willing to provide what she needed, for the sake of her protection and his soon-to-be granddaughter's. "Should you call him to tell him we're coming? I can load the minutes on the phone."

"He's never met Lily. And of course, he's never even heard of you." She hesitated, pinching her lips. "No. No phone call. He lives in a fancy gated community on the north side of Indianapolis, so the guard on duty will call him and he'll have to approve us. It'll be a lot harder for him to turn us away if we're there already and there's a gossipy guard watching his every move. I don't like to push him like that, but I don't think we have any other choice."

Reid scrubbed his hand over his chin stubble. There might be one other place they could seek help, but it was quite a ways outside Indy, and it wasn't a relationship he wanted to have to depend on again. The last time he had seen the man he called Bump, Reid had promised him that life would be different. Better. "So which way?"

"Head to I-465, and take it around to the Keystone exit."

Reid pushed on his sunglasses as he turned the vehicle into the late-afternoon sun. Thomas Callahan was the most sought-after divorce attorney in the greater Indianapolis area. Reid had no intention of ever becoming a divorce lawyer, but being in the man's good books could go a long way toward a successful practice. He must have connections all over central Indiana. Reid's heartbeat picked up a notch at the thought of Mr. Callahan's reaction to his daughter's current circumstances. What would the man think when he found out about the attempted kidnapping of his daughter and her ward?

ELEVEN

Samantha's weekend plans had been completely demolished. She could accept that.

But as she lowered the visor against the setting summer sun, it seemed that her very life was speeding by like the businesses and homes at each exit of the interstate that looped around Indianapolis. She would never take Lily for granted again. She would do everything in her power to make a wonderful life for the girl. Family dinners. Vacations. Heart-to-heart girl talks. She would savor every normal moment that came her way.

She snuck a glance at Reid, stoic and absorbed in his own thoughts as he steered his Jeep toward a door Samantha hadn't thought she'd darken for a while longer. What would normal moments be like with Reid? What if he was a part of making that wonderful life?

She choked on the thought, sputtering and reaching for her raspberry tea.

"You okay?" Reid's baritone snagged at her. Did he really care? Did this man who had gotten himself kicked out of law school really care about anyone besides himself?

She sipped, letting the cool liquid soothe her ragged throat. "Fine."

Of course he could. He had protected them so far. She couldn't deny that. But what about once the bad guys were caught? She would go back to work. Lily would start school soon. And Reid? He would go forward with his plans, whatever they were. And whatever they were, they didn't include her.

They better not include her. There was no way God would send her another bad boy. No way. If she needed anyone at all, and so far she hadn't, she wanted it to be a good, safe, reliable man. One who was steady and secure. As far as she could tell, there wasn't one within a hundred-mile radius.

Reid didn't have any of those qualities.

Or did he? So far, Reid hadn't exhibited any similarities to the man he used to be.

"Do I call him Grandpa?"

Lily's timid question startled Samantha out of her thoughts. She focused on the supercenter as they whizzed past another interstate exit, trying to regain her bearings. Based on the street name at the exit, she figured they had another twenty minutes or so. Plenty of time to worry about showing up on her father's doorstep with two strangers in tow.

Samantha held her open chocolate bar up to her nose and inhaled deeply of the bitter sweetness. Perhaps just the aroma would get those endorphins flowing and the sensation of relaxation started.

"I guess he's not legally my grandpa yet, is he? Do I call him Mr. Callahan?"

The girl had a valid question. One that Samantha hadn't yet considered. "Well, eventually you'll call him Grandpa. But for right now, why don't we leave it up to him? Sound okay?"

"Yeah. Is he nice? Will he like me?"

Without taking his eyes off the highway, Reid turned his head slightly toward Samantha. He raised his eyebrows as if he wanted to ask if her father would like him. Anxiety with the weight of an anvil pressed on Samantha's shoulders, and she slumped in her seat. She had no idea what her father would think of either Lily or Reid. She only knew that a few years ago, he hadn't had any interest in family life. She had no reason to think that had changed.

"Right or left up here?"

She'd been navel-gazing again. Samantha forced her eyes to focus on the name of the street ahead as she gave Reid the rest of the directions. Soon they pulled up to a matched set of stone lions that guarded the stately entrance to the gated community. A rock formation with a melodious waterfall was flanked by a profusion of multicolored flowers, and a manicured golf course beckoned to the west.

Reid pulled up to the guardhouse and lowered his window. "Samantha Callahan is here for Thomas Callahan." Samantha leaned toward Reid's window and waved at the guard.

"Yes, sir. Ma'am." The guard flipped through a book then picked up a landline phone.

As the guard talked to her father, Samantha leaned on the middle console to see into the hut. The clean scent of Reid's shirt filled her senses, the stubble of his strong chin standing out in relief against the evening sun. Where would she be right now without Reid's protection? Where would Lily be? She shuddered to think of it.

A moment later, the guard hung up. He pushed a button inside the guardhouse and the gate began to swing open. "Mr. Callahan is expecting you."

"Thank you." Samantha settled back in her seat as Reid pulled through the gate. Soon, it would clang shut behind them. But would it be to enclose them in safety or to entrap them with no way out?

As they pulled into her father's driveway, the front door opened and her father stepped out. Dapper in khaki trousers and a dark green golf shirt, he raised a hand in greeting as if posing for an advertisement to welcome guests to the neighborhood. Samantha narrowed her eyes at him, but his smile looked genuine.

"Samantha, I'm glad you're here." Her father's voice boomed across the yard.

The hair on her arms prickled. Did he have a woman friend there he was trying to impress? She couldn't remember the last time she'd had a greeting like that from the man she called Dad.

Reid looked at her, seemingly waiting for her to make the first move, then his eyes darted around the property. "Everything look all right to you?"

She couldn't fault him for being on constant surveillance. In fact, she appreciated his protectiveness. She glanced around the front of the house and the lawn. "Looks the same as last time."

She squeaked the car door open and heard Lily's door open behind her. A small hand wormed its way into hers, and she grasped it, seeking to comfort the girl as much as she sought comfort for herself. As she rounded the front of the Jeep, Reid emerged from the driver's seat and accompanied her up the walk.

"Hi, Dad." Samantha cleared her throat. "Thanks for letting us stop by." She stood still, waiting for that awkward moment of realization that her father wasn't going to hug her, even though that was what most dads would do.

Reid stepped forward, hand outstretched. Samantha took a tiny step back. God bless that man for rescuing her...again. "Good evening, sir. I'm Reid Palmer. Your daughter and I were classmates in law school, and we sort of ran into each other the other day, so I gave her a ride here."

Well, he certainly had left a lot out. A lot that she would have to explain in the very near future.

Her father was at least cordial enough to shake Reid's hand, but the congeniality quickly slid from his countenance as he studied Samantha. A frown crept into its place. Samantha watched his attention dart between them until he settled on her. She looked down at her front, smoothing out the rumples on her shirt, and then running a hand over her hair. She must look rather disheveled. "Is this your boyfriend? I can't say I'm impressed with how you're keeping yourself. Perhaps he's not the right one for you."

Suddenly he was concerned with her well-being? Whatever conversation needed to take place, it shouldn't happen in the front yard, not with a couple of guys after them with the uncanny ability to track them no matter where they went. Samantha held up a hand. "Dad, he's not my boyfriend. Like Reid said, we only ran into each other yesterday. Actually, I ran into him, but that comes earlier in the story." She surveyed the street and pulled Lily a little closer. "Can we come in, and I'll tell you the whole thing?"

"As long as you're here…" He backed up slowly, then turned and led them into the house.

As the door closed behind them, Reid turned for one last look out front. Then he nodded to Samantha, indicating that all seemed well.

For now.

Her dad showed them to the well-appointed living room decorated in shades of dark blue and brown. A baseball game played on the television, and he hit the mute button on the remote. Samantha moved to sit, and Lily popped out from her hiding place behind Samantha.

Apparently, the surprises weren't over for Thomas Callahan. "Who's this?" He raised his eyebrows at Samantha. "I know it's been a while since I've seen you, and I'm sorry about that. But it hasn't been long enough for you to have a baby who's grown up."

"Dad, this is Lily. Her parents have both passed on, and her father appointed me as guardian."

"Well, this pretty thing is practically a young lady." He smiled at Lily and held out his hand. Lily stepped toward him and gently placed her hand in his. A smile erupted on Lily's face, and she sidled up next to Samantha's dad. "How old are you, pumpkin?"

Samantha jerked back, wrinkling her nose. *Pumpkin?* Never in her entire life had she heard her father use a term of affection. What was going on?

Lily's smile threatened to tear her face in half. "I'm ten, sir."

"Sir? We can't have that." Her dad stroked his chin as if deep in thought. "Let's see. What shall you call me? What about Granddad? Grandpa? Gramps? You choose."

"I like Grandpa."

"Then, Grandpa it is." He gestured toward the kitchen. "Why don't you run in there and get yourself a can of pop?" He turned to Samantha. "If you say it's okay."

Samantha fought hard not to grimace. Who

was this man, and what had he done with her father? It was like one of those bad movies where everyone switches bodies. She forced herself to take a breath. "Sure. Fine."

As her father watched Lily go into the kitchen, Samantha turned to Reid and shrugged her shoulders. She had no idea why her father was so different.

With Lily safely stowed away, her dad turned a serious look to her. "So what's going on?"

Reid tamped down the desire to sit next to Samantha and take her hand. Something to provide support and encouragement. She had the nervous look of someone on the witness stand. But if he consoled her like he wanted to, her father would feel certain that they were romantically involved, and Reid definitely didn't want to add that complication to Samantha's already difficult relationship with her father.

What he really wanted was to figure out who was behind this chase. The police were doing what they could, but that was actually quite limited. These thugs were good and didn't leave evidence behind. Apparently, if they didn't want to be found, they wouldn't be. Maybe, with the use of Mr. Callahan's computer, they could at least learn about the company Lily's father had worked for and figure out what was on that flash drive that Lily's father had given to his daughter in his final days. Instead, he and Samantha were stuck explaining themselves to their only hope for a new vehicle and some cash.

As Samantha stammered through her explanation of their current circumstances, Reid paced at the end of the sofa. He tried to adopt what he hoped was a kind and caring expression every time Thomas Callahan shot a look of suspicion his way. He needed to do something to convince her father, and Samantha herself, that his intentions were honorable. And if that something removed him from their presence, then all the better.

Water. That was it. She needed ice water. "Mr. Callahan, may I get a glass of ice water for Samantha? I'm sure she could use some cool refreshment."

Her father plastered on a smile that Reid was sure had convinced many divorcees of his sincerity. But Thomas's eyes glinted with cold calculation. "Of course. And call me Thomas. There's no need for formality." He gestured toward the kitchen, his gold pinkie ring shimmering in the recessed lights. "Glasses are in the cabinet next to the refrigerator."

"Thank you." Reid felt as though he should

bow formally as he left the man's presence. Instead, he offered a slight grin to Samantha and moved to the kitchen.

Lily sat at the counter, sipping her pop and thumbing through a cookbook full of photos of gourmet meals. It wouldn't be long before she uttered her famous words, *I'm hungry.*

"Hey, munchkin. How do you feel?" He found the cupboard and retrieved a large clear glass.

"I'm bored. Can I watch a movie or something?"

"It's not my house, but I would think so, after Samantha's done talking to her father." He pulled the freezer door open and dropped a couple handfuls of ice cubes in the glass. The clink of the cubes against each other satisfied him, as if he were actually accomplishing something. Frigid air from the freezer blew the heat of pressure off his face.

Despite the wealthy elegance of the home, it was not all that spacious. Reid could hear nearly every word Thomas uttered to his daughter in the adjoining living room. As he waited, he checked his watch against the clock on the oven. Thomas had been interrogating his daughter like a hostile witness for at least a half hour, and all possible conversation topics had been exhausted. By now, the man must understand their position and their limited courses of action.

Reid raised his hand, ready to slap the counter, but checked himself. A display of frustration wouldn't help them plead their case to Thomas.

If Samantha wouldn't do it, he would have to. It was now or never. He would ask her dad if they could borrow a vehicle since the thugs were looking for Reid's Jeep. Asking for money would take another level of courage.

But losing a position of authority due to his own foolishness had taken the edge off his bravado and knocked him to his knees. Summoning his strength and squaring his shoulders, he tried to turn back to the living room, but his feet wouldn't move. Just then, Thomas's voice softened. "I need a drink," he said to Samantha. "And I'll check on your water."

"Thanks," she answered, and the next moment Reid felt a strong hand clap him on the shoulder.

Thomas murmured under his breath right behind Reid, "Thank you for keeping my daughter safe."

"Uh, sure." A foot stepped behind him, and Reid turned to see genuine softness in Thomas's expression. What had he missed while he'd been stuck in his own thoughts? What—

ever it was, he wouldn't question it. He'd just accept it.

Thomas pulled a glass from the cabinet and poured some iced tea. "Do you have enough cash, son? The ladies can be expensive." He tilted his head toward the living room where his daughter sat with her head bowed as if in prayer.

"It's really not like that, sir. We just need to be able to cover basic expenses, like food and gas, while we try to figure this out."

Thomas pulled out his wallet and opened it wide enough for Reid to glance a sturdy stash of bills. He selected two bills and handed Reid a couple hundred dollars. "Take my car, too. They'll be looking for yours, right? I have a sweet little SUV in the third car garage. I'm not sure why I bought it, since it's not something I normally drive, so take it. Let's pull your Jeep into the garage to hide it."

Huh?

Something odd was going on, because this was not the man Samantha described.

Thomas leaned back against the counter. "So what kind of work do you do? I figure you know something about weapons and self-defense after what Samantha has told me."

Reid ran a hand through his hair. "After college, I got into the police academy, ambitious to right society's wrongs. I was an officer for a few years. Then I left the force to go to law school."

"Another way to right wrongs?"

"Something like that." Bile rising from his stomach threatened to choke him. Samantha's father would kick him to the curb if he knew Reid's history. No father would want their daughter anywhere close to the son of an abuser, particularly one who had exhibited plenty of difficulty handling anger himself. Something in Reid's gut told him that the divorce lawyer didn't allow for second chances. If Thomas asked straight out, Reid would have to answer truthfully, no matter how humiliating or shameful that would be. He wouldn't lie. But he didn't have an obligation to tell all. No one dumped their entire history on a brand-new acquaintance. It wouldn't be expected, nor was it appropriate. Lots of past difficulties just never got shared.

Especially since these particular relationships with Samantha and her father would be so short-lived.

It was time for a change of subject, to something actually helpful. "Sir, can I use your computer? I'd like to see if I can find out any more about Lily's father and his employer. We also found a flash drive hidden in a key chain. Need to find out what's on it."

Thomas studied him for a moment as if trying to decipher his expression. Then the moment broke, and Thomas gestured to another room. "Sure. It's in the den. Just off the living room."

"Grandpa?" Lily was still in the kitchen. Her timid voice sounded as if it was trying on a shirt two sizes too big.

"What can I do for you, sweetie?" Thomas smiled for her, a portrait of a loving and involved grandfather.

"Can I watch a movie?"

"Mr. Palmer and I have some business, so ask your, uh, Samantha, to find something for you on TV. Okay?"

The strains of kid-friendly music soon filtered into the den as Thomas joined Reid at the computer.

Reid typed in *Zigfried Pharmaceuticals*. "We've been wondering if this has something to do with Lily's father. He was killed not long ago in what seemed like a regular car accident, but now I'm not so sure. He worked at Zigfried, so maybe there's some connection there."

The Zigfried Pharmaceuticals home page came up, but Reid couldn't find any sort of employee directory. He clicked on a link labeled Executive Officers. Another webpage included photos and brief bios of the president, various vice presidents and assorted research heads. "There doesn't seem to be any information on other employees. Only the bigwigs. I suppose there are too many and they're too transitional."

Thomas pointed at a picture on the screen of a debonair man with salt-and-pepper hair. "I handled the divorce for this senior vice president a couple of years ago. As part of the division of marital property, he had to provide his private financials." He chuckled. "That was when I got the SUV you're going to borrow." He straightened and shook his head as if he'd just realized the timing of the case to the vehicle purchase. "I can tell you a lot of money changes hands at that company. But that doesn't necessarily have any bearing on your current situation."

"So another dead end. We're no closer to an answer." Reid clicked away from the company's site and crossed his arms over his chest.

"What about the girl's extended family members?" Thomas dropped into a wing chair in the corner. "Grandparents? Aunts or uncles? Any greats? You might be surprised at who crawls out of the woodwork to assert themselves or demand something when there's a family upset."

Reid suppressed an urge to respond that he knew a few things about the law, too. "I don't know anything about Lily's family. But that's a good point. I read some pretty wild cases in law school."

"Samantha said that both parents were deceased, and it sounded as though she only knew the father. The girl going to a virtual family stranger would certainly fall under the definition of a family upset in my book." Thomas rose and stepped to the door to call Samantha from the living room.

She appeared in the doorway, straightening her shirt about her waist, unasked questions creasing her delicate brow. Reid's heart thumped at her appearance. It had been less than an hour since he had interacted with her last, but apparently his heart thought it had been too long. He turned back to the computer. This was getting dangerous, and not just because a couple of thugs were after them.

"I don't want to upset the girl, so let's talk in here," Thomas said. "I wondered if she might have any extended family that could be behind this attempted kidnapping. Maybe someone who is upset that her father made you guardian?"

Reid swiveled back to Samantha and Thomas, fighting to maintain what he hoped was a neutral expression.

Samantha tapped a finger on her lips before she spoke. "She doesn't have much family. That's why I'm her guardian. There's a great-aunt, but her health isn't good. She wouldn't be able to care for Lily."

"And yet another dead end." Reid's stomach growled. Samantha's stomach harmonized with its own rumble.

Thomas raised his eyebrows and chuckled. "I don't keep much food around, since I go out a lot for business and with, ahem, friends. But why don't we order a couple of pizzas? Use my credit card." He looked up at Reid's height with a smile. "You look as though you could pack away an entire pizza by yourself."

"That sounds terrific, Dad. I'm sure Lily's hungry, too."

"Hold up." Reid held out a hand. "I'm not sure that's best. Credit card use might give away our location, depending on the resources of the guy directing the thugs. Samantha, since you and your father share a last name and you're both attorneys, it wouldn't be hard to connect you two. I did."

Thomas pulled his card out of his wallet. "That would take a pretty high level of sophistication with technology, Reid. I'll use my own credit card and my own name, and Samantha's name will never be attached to any of it. And remember that gate at the entrance to the subdivision? No one comes in unless approved. I'll have to call the guard and let him know that a pizza delivery from my favorite restaurant will be coming. It'll be fine." He clapped Reid on the back, but the gesture didn't provide the reassurance it had before in the kitchen.

Thomas quickly placed the two calls, one to the pizza place and the other to the guard, then turned to smile at Samantha and Reid. "No problem. A few minutes and we'll be scarfing down sausage and pepperoni. I can smell it already." He left them alone in the den. A moment later, the couch cushions sighed and Reid heard him ask Lily how she liked the show.

Samantha stepped a little farther into the room and leaned against the wall, dark clouds of consternation gathering across her brow. "So now you and my dad are best buds?" she whispered. "You're doing that male-bonding thing?"

"I'm not sure what you mean by 'that male-bonding thing,' but once you explained what was going on, he seemed like a nice guy. I don't doubt you've had a difficult time with him. But maybe he's changing. Reforming."

Mr. Callahan's behavior had perplexed him, but people in transition from wrongs to rights often displayed confusing behavior as they wobbled in between the bad and the good. "In my years as a police officer, I picked up, or maybe I learned, a sixth sense about people's real motivations. Who they really are. Your father seems regretful for his past actions. I have no idea why, but maybe he wants to turn over a new leaf with you and your sister."

"Oh, come on. You really expect me to believe that? People don't just change spontaneously."

"Anyone can change, with the power of God." He was living proof. But Samantha's blue eyes only tossed sparks of fire. "You honestly can't see any difference in me or in your father?"

She sagged, hugging her arms around her middle and staring at the floor. "You're right. I can. And you're right that God can do anything, especially with someone who wants to do His will."

He crossed the space between them and, with one hand on her shoulder, tipped her chin so she would look up at him. "Was that so difficult to admit?"

"It's barely been twenty-four hours since I rear-ended your Jeep, but I can tell you're a different person since we were in law school together. You seemed so rebellious then. Now you're stable. Dependable. All qualities that make you even more handsome." She gasped and her hand flew up to cover her mouth.

She thought he was handsome? Without hesitation, he pulled her hand away and leaned down, one focus consuming him: her soft lips. But a loud blare of music from the movie in the other room startled her, and she stepped back. "No, I can't trust again. I'm sorry. Forget I said anything."

Reid returned to the chair, feeling as though an anvil was sitting on his chest. He had put himself out there, risked his heart and been rejected without even a moment's consideration. His chest might burn now, but it would fade to a dull ache. "I'm sorry I made you uncomfortable. All is forgotten." He muttered the words, but could he convince his heart?

The best thing to do was focus on the tasks ahead. He retrieved the flash drive and plugged it into the laptop. "One last thing to check. Let's see what's on here."

He clicked on the drive for the removable disk when it popped up, and the screen filled with file names. A click on the first one brought up a spreadsheet with columns of names and corresponding numbers that looked like social security numbers. Another column listed dollar amounts ranging from a couple thousand to over one hundred thousand. The other files on the flash drive contained similar information, including account numbers and bank statements.

Samantha leaned over his shoulder, her hair tickling his neck. "What is it?"

"I think it's evidence of embezzlement. I don't know much about financial crimes, but it looks as if someone has been moving money around."

"Lily's father?"

"No. Probably the guy who has those thugs after us. I'm guessing Lily's father found this evidence, hid a copy on the flash drive, and that's what got him killed."

"Can you tell from those files who he is?"

Reid clicked and scanned and clicked and scanned. "No. No idea. Most likely it was someone with access to the company financials, but I don't know past that."

"So what now?"

"This is beyond the scope of the Heartwood Hill Police Department, but let's email a copy to Derek for safekeeping. Let's email a copy to you, as well."

Samantha placed a hand on Reid's shoulder

but quickly withdrew it. "Are we a step closer to ending this chase, then?"

Before he could log in to his email account, Lily bounded into the room. "Pizza's on its way." She pulled on Reid's arm. "Come on, Mr. Palmer, I want you to see this really funny part of the show."

The girl had good timing, giving him an out. "All right. Just a minute." He ejected the flash drive and pocketed it, then followed Lily toward the door. Samantha didn't look up as he passed. "I'll email after we eat. Okay?"

She only nodded, and he left the room, leaving all hope of a relationship behind, as well.

TWELVE

Samantha leaned her head against the wall as the breeze created by Reid's sudden departure left her chilled. She hugged her arms around her middle. The lack of his presence created a vacuum of emotion. What did she feel toward him? Yes, she wished he was still in the room, but was that because of the way his T-shirt stretched across his broad shoulders? Or was it because of his protection and the way he had saved her life many times over? What about the way his dark eyes had flashed both conviction and warmth at his insistence that people could change? Or worse yet...was it all of the above?

And what about her father? Why did he care so much? She punched herself in the arm to chastise herself for her disrespectful attitude. Her father had never been callous toward her or uncaring. Just too selfish to be all that involved. But now he definitely seemed interested. Why? It wasn't disrespectful—it was a valid question.

If there was anything she had learned in law school, it was to ask questions.

But that was a question that most likely wouldn't get answered before they had pizza, and probably not at all. She turned off the light and spun on her heel to head to the kitchen.

Lily sat enthroned between Samantha's father and Reid. Reid refused to look up at her as she brushed past, deliberately stepping around him so as not to make contact in any way.

"Dad, can I make a salad to go with the pizza?" She stood in the middle of the walkway into the kitchen, hesitant to pry into his cabinets and refrigerator.

Without taking his eyes from the screen, he waved her toward the kitchen, seemingly unaware that she was already in there. "I'm not sure what I have in the fridge, but help yourself."

She wasn't sure what could be so captivating for her father in the movie, especially the current scene of a couple of adolescent girls, twins even, sitting alone at a table in a dining hall. It had been her and her sister's favorite movie when they were younger, the story of twins separated by their parents' divorce, then reunited at a summer camp and ultimately able to reunite their parents. But her father hadn't ever been interested...until now.

Hmm. Maybe he would get some ideas. Ideas about reconciliation with his ex-wife. Ideas about how to be an involved father. Samantha opened the refrigerator. But probably not.

The vegetable drawer looked generally unused, except for a small bag of prepackaged chopped lettuce, the kind with bits of carrot and cabbage, and a half container of cherry tomatoes. She set those on the counter and rummaged in the cabinets until she found a crystal bowl. Her mother had taught her that if she didn't have enough to go around, she ought at least to put it in a pretty dish. The lettuce was rather white and anemic, and there were only a dozen little tomatoes, but at least it all sparkled in the bowl.

She searched for tongs but when she came up empty, she settled on a couple of forks. She placed the bowl on the breakfast bar, unsure what to do next. She wanted to check her email and her social media. See if she had received the documents a client had promised to send. Check her mail for the latest edition of her favorite legal journal. Put her feet up and relax with a good legal suspense novel.

But instead she was trapped inside her father's house, her life tossed just like that salad. Turned upside down by some thugs who wanted her or Lily or both of them. Her faith should be the crystal bowl, making her sparkle, but too often, she felt tarnished.

As she reached into another cabinet for plates and glasses, the doorbell rang, heralding the arrival of the pizza.

"Woo-hoo!" Lily held up her hand for a high-five from Samantha's father. "Pizza's here!"

Her dad jumped up from the sofa, returned the high-five and headed toward the front door.

Reid stood slowly, flashing a warning look to Samantha. "Sir? The guard at the gatehouse didn't call you."

Her dad waved him off. "Yeah, he knew we were having pizza delivered. No need."

As she arranged the table service on the bar, Reid shrugged but stayed close behind her father. Samantha came out from behind the kitchen counter, ready to serve up the hot meal.

Her dad opened the door as he reached into his pants pocket and retrieved a couple of bills. Probably two twenties, although that would more than cover the cost of the pizza and provide a generous tip. He held them out to the delivery guy, a large man with a ball cap pulled down over his eyes, the logo of the pizza company emblazoned on the front.

As Reid stepped forward and to the side of her father, Samantha saw a glint of metal under the pizza boxes that nearly made her heart stop beating. She sucked in her breath, a sound that made Reid turn to her. At seeing her expression, he turned back toward the door to follow her line of sight.

It was a gun. The pizza delivery guy balanced the pizza boxes on a gun he held pointed at her father.

Panic grabbed Samantha by the neck and held her still, unable even to swallow.

Like a cat springing on a field mouse, Reid leaped for her dad. He grabbed him around the shoulders, pulling him back from the door and toward a corner in the little hallway.

The thug shoved the pizza boxes toward Reid. A snarl emanated from his throat as sauce and pepperoni and cheese flew from the box onto her father and then dropped onto the tile floor.

A horrific popping sound filled Samantha's ears. The gun went off as Reid and her father dived behind a wall in the foyer. A profusion of bright red burst from her father's leg. He crumpled to the ground, the twenties in his hand fluttering down as if in slow motion.

Reid pulled her father behind the wall and

pulled his own weapon out of the ankle holster. "Get down!" he called to Samantha.

The man in the pizza delivery hat spotted Reid's weapon and dived into the bushes just outside the front door. Samantha dropped to the floor, peering around the end cabinet as Reid elbow crawled to the front door. He slammed it shut, then stretched up to jam the dead bolt into place.

The salad in the bowl fell off the breakfast bar as she wobbled on her ankles, flailing against the front of the cabinet to keep her balance. The bowl fell with a terrific crash, and she startled as if another shot had been fired. She watched the tomatoes roll across the floor, unable to blink, until she forced her attention back and swung her gaze to Lily, who was on her knees at the end of the sofa.

Were they safe now? Or would he shoot the lock off the door? Break a window? Come in the back?

Silence reigned for a moment, save for the pained gasps of her father. Her gaze locked on Lily. She refused to look away, willing comfort and love and a promise of security through the connection.

A throaty whisper filtered through her concentration. It was Reid. "Get Lily. Get to your dad's SUV."

Her father tried to sit up. "Keys are on the hook. Near the garage door."

How could she go? Didn't Reid realize what he was asking her to do? Where would she go without his guidance and protection? And what about her dad? He was shot and in desperate need of medical attention. "I'm not leaving you. Either of you."

Reid exchanged a knowing look with her father. "You're not leaving me. Back out, and I'll catch you in the driveway."

Lily appeared by her side as the first tear slid down Samantha's cheek. "What about Dad? He took a bullet for me. For us. He needs help."

Her father managed to smile around a wince of pain. "Go. Run. Stay with Reid. He'll take care of you." He nodded to Reid as if he already knew Reid's plan. When he looked back at Samantha, his eyes were filled with tears. "I love you."

How could this be happening? Her father actually had said he loved her, and now she had to leave him in a puddle of his own blood as she escaped for her life? Lily had to leave Grandpa nearly as soon as she had met him?

"Go!"

The fog shrouding her mind didn't allow her to know who was telling her to go, but she instinctively obeyed. She grabbed Lily's hand and pulled her up and down the hallway toward the garage. The key was labeled and hung right where her father said it would be.

She swung the door open, listening to the men's muffled voices. Her father was wounded, and she was now thrust again into the care of a man she still wasn't sure she trusted. They had gone to her father for safety, and now she and Lily were going to be on the run again. She stepped into the dark garage and tightened her grip on Lily's hand. Then she swung the door shut on the little bit of security she had known for just a short time and turned into the inky blackness.

Reid groaned, his tone mingling with the muffled moans of Samantha's father. They had brought trouble to Thomas, big trouble, and Reid was the only one to blame. He had pushed Samantha into it.

He slapped his hand on his own cheek. There was no time for feeling sorry now. Regret would arrive with its full effect in its own time, lingering like an unwelcome guest. Right now, he had to dial nine-one-one on his way out.

Reid grabbed the phone from the kitchen and hit the numbers, then handed it to Thomas, where he sat against the wall around the corner from the foyer. "I called for help. Can you give them directions?"

"Yes." Pain forced Thomas's voice into a grunt. "There's a gun. On top of the refrigerator. In the planter."

Reid rushed for the kitchen and dug around in the pot of the artificial plant. The handle of a weapon protruded from the fake moss. He couldn't help but grin at the clever hiding place as he handed the weapon to Thomas.

Thomas laid it on the floor next to him. "I'll be fine. Go help my daughter. My granddaughter." He shifted his position with a groan of pain then pierced Reid with an intense stare. "And thank you for keeping her alive."

Without further goodbyes, Reid turned and ran for the garage. Inside, in the disappearing light of the closing door, he made for the side door. He rushed out to the driveway. Samantha was at the wheel of the little SUV, panic streaked across her face. As she slowly backed down the driveway, Reid ran for the passenger door. When he catapulted himself inside the vehicle, Samantha yelped in surprise.

He crouched low in the seat, as best he could for a man of his height, and watched the front yard. The front door was still closed. Reid breathed with relief that that meant Thomas was still safe. But as Samantha threw the vehicle into Drive, one of the now familiar ruffians raced from the bushes near the street and toward a large dark-colored SUV at another house down the road.

Reid turned to the front, trying to remember how to get out of the subdivision. Samantha huddled behind the wheel, seemingly too afraid to think straight.

"Drive!" He couldn't help but bark out the command. "Turn right up here. Get back to the main road."

Samantha gripped the wheel, her fright etched in the lines around her narrowed eyes. "What about my dad? I can't leave him." But she pressed on the accelerator, and the SUV jumped forward.

"He's fine. I called for help. He has a gun." Reid spun to see the bad guys gaining on them. "These guys don't want your dad. They'll leave him alone." Especially since they were drawing them away and into a chase, but that didn't need to be said out loud.

As sirens wailed in the distance, Samantha relaxed her shoulders. She turned toward the exit of the community as Reid withdrew his weapon from the holster.

"What about the gate? Won't it be down?" Samantha swiped at her forehead then stuck her hand back on the wheel.

The gate. He'd forgotten about that. "Don't stop. Just drive through it."

Samantha turned to him for a split second. "Seriously?"

"There's no other choice." With his left hand, he gripped her right arm and squeezed confidence into her. "You've got this."

She adjusted her hands on the wheel and squared her shoulders, a fierce determination radiating from her. "Lily, get down."

The black SUV squealed its tires as it gunned around the corner behind them. Samantha leaned into the accelerator, heading straight for the gate. Reid's stare collided with the security guard's, who seemed immobile in the pending danger. Apologies and repairs could be made later. Right now, it was the gate or their lives.

The little SUV hit the gate at a terrific speed. The flimsy metal structure popped off its hinges and flung into the boxwoods and impatiens. Samantha turned onto the deserted main road, the black SUV close behind.

A moment later, the SUV caught up and veered into the adjacent lane. As they drove side by side, the thug in the passenger seat lowered his window and hollered at them, "Pull over!" The barrel of a gun stared at them from the SUV.

Reid leaned in close to Samantha's ear, his weapon held below the window. "Keep driving. They won't shoot us because they want you alive for something."

The black SUV sideswiped them, and metal grated on metal. Samantha gripped the wheel to hold their vehicle steady, but her foot must have relaxed on the accelerator because the little SUV began to slow down.

"Don't stop!" Reid longed to jump in the driver's seat, but that was impossible now. He had a plan, if only Samantha could keep going for a couple more minutes.

She grimaced as she stared straight ahead. "You really think I would?"

Reid visually confirmed that Lily was still down on the floor of the backseat as he instructed Samantha. "Get back as much as you can."

She pressed her back into the seat, the strain of the effort telling on her face. "I can only go so far."

"It's fine. As they pull up to us again, veer away a little."

As the SUVs lined up again, Reid brought his weapon up right in front of her and aimed through the window. The world seemed to slow in motion as he tilted the barrel down and fired at the front passenger tire. With the acrid smell of gunpowder filling his nostrils, he shot at the rear tire.

Samantha screeched, probably at the blast of the weapon being discharged right in front of her. The SUV's tires immediately deflated, the sound of the rubber flapping against the pavement following Reid and Samantha as they sped away. Reid swiveled to see out the back window. The thug in the passenger side leaned out the open window, aiming his gun at them. A shot was fired, and Reid ducked. But the big SUV careened wildly with the disabled tires, and the bullet shot into the trees.

"Are they gone? Is it over?" Samantha continued driving down the main road, keeping a steady speed.

"Can I get up?" Lily's muffled voice filtered from the backseat.

Reid sagged into the passenger seat and finally buckled his seat belt. "Yes. We're fine." His heart rate slowed as he gulped in deep breaths. When his muscles had relaxed to a normal tension, he smiled at Samantha. "You should try to qualify for the Indianapolis 500."

Samantha shot him an amused look. "Sure. Funny man." She paused, and her expression turned to distress. "While you're making jokes, my father is lying on the floor of his house with a bullet in his leg. What about that?"

Did she really think he didn't know that? His stomach tightened along with his fists. What had he just done for her? He fought the urge to smash his fist into the dashboard and filled his mind with prayer instead. *Lord, help.* That would have to do, because it was all he could muster. He filled his lungs with one more cleansing breath before he dared to answer her. "Did you not hear the sirens? I called nine-one-one, and left your father with his gun. He knew he'd be fine and urged me to go with you. To help you."

"Maybe I don't need help. Maybe Lily and I would be fine without you."

"What? I've saved you and Lily from kidnapping and who knows what else now how many times? You want to go it alone? Fine. Drop me off at the nearest Chinese restaurant." Never mind the fact that his Jeep now sat in Thomas Callahan's driveway. He could walk. Anything to be on his own again.

Samantha swung her gaze from side to side as if looking for a place to drop him. He let his shoulders sag and pulled the burner cell from his pocket. At the very least, he should call Derek to update him. After that, they could use that cell maybe one more time, and then they should ditch it and get another to avoid being traced.

Samantha fixed her gaze at him, an unasked question arching her delicate eyebrows.

"I'm calling my buddy on the force to let him know what's happened. We're out of Heartwood Hill's jurisdiction, but Derek will want to coordinate with local law enforcement. I doubt they'll get to the site before those guys can change their tires and get out of there, but they'll want to try. Those thugs are good, and they'll be prepared for anything." He held his thumb over the keypad.

"Reid." She paused to chew on her bottom lip. "It's too late for any Chinese restaurant to be open. I think you'll just have to stick with me."

"Is that an apology?"

"I wouldn't call it that, but if that'll soothe your pride—"

"My pride? Listen, I'm not just trying to be a hero. All I'm doing—"

She laid her hand on his arm, a whisper of a touch that left him oddly calmed. One minute, she ruffled his feathers. The next, he wanted to gather her in his arms and assure her that all would be well. That he would be there until the very end. But not only was that embrace not physically possible with her behind the wheel, it wouldn't be the best option for either of their hearts.

"I'm just a little overwhelmed with everything that's happened. I don't quite understand what happened back there with my dad, but it seemed that our relationship was on the mend, even if it was just for tonight. And then he was injured protecting me. Reid, he was shot. I've never seen anyone get shot before, let alone a family member. I just don't know if his change is genuine, and then to have to race out into the night and leave him there…"

"The ambulance is there by now, and judging by the location of the wound, he'll most likely be fine. You can call the hospital later to check on him." That would be a risk, but one they would probably have to take.

He pressed his hand to his chest. The bigger risk suddenly seemed to be what she was doing to his heart.

THIRTEEN

The dark of the night enveloped the little SUV, broken only by pale circles created by passing streetlights. The hour on the clock was not yet midnight, but it was late enough that as Reid watched the little suburb out his passenger-side window, the shops were dark and restaurants signaled they were closed with upended chair legs silhouetted in the windows.

Reid scratched at the stubble on his chin. Since he had met Samantha Callahan, safety had become a rarity. For the moment, since their attackers were disabled by flat tires, safety was their companion. But how far down the road would those guys with malicious intent catch up?

He dialed the burner cell for Derek, the one man on the force who seemed to hold no ill will regarding his past indiscretions. As the phone rang, he glanced at Samantha. He couldn't quite read her expression, but her breathing was steady and seemed to be calm. Lily, in the backseat, had leaned her head against the headrest and was breathing like someone almost asleep. She seemed to be handling all this with grace and humor, but that could be because she didn't quite grasp the seriousness of the situation. What could a ten-year-old girl, raised in a loving and protective family, know or understand about running for safety? What a terrible introduction to the evil in the world.

A sleepy voice answered the phone. "Yeah? Whatever this is, it better be worth it."

Reid wanted to slap his hand on his forehead. Of course Derek wouldn't know who was calling since it was a burner phone. "It's me, Reid. Thanks for picking up, Derek."

Sheets rustled in the background. Derek must have sat up for he sounded more alert. "What's up?"

"Had a little run-in with those guys again. We went to Samantha's father's house, thinking it was safe. But they found us there when her father ordered a pizza. Her dad got shot. I called nine-one-one and he's probably at the hospital already. We got away, but only because I shot out their tires. Might want to see if they're still on the side of the road, but it's doubtful." He described the location where the big SUV might still be.

"Are you two, you three, all right?"

"We're fine. Samantha's a little shaken up." He glanced at Samantha to see her nod her head in agreement.

"I'll talk to Local and see who's out there. But, Reid?"

The cautious tone in Derek's voice made the hair on the back of Reid's neck stand up. "Yeah?"

"You might want to know that not all the guys here are as glad to see you back as I am."

"I figured. Our first encounter with Cody on desk duty wasn't exactly pleasant."

"They probably just need a little time to come around."

Reid rubbed a hand over the back of his neck. This was what he had expected, but to actually hear the words? "You should also know that we're not in my Jeep anymore. Samantha's father, Thomas Callahan, the well-known lawyer, let us borrow his vehicle. The uniforms on the scene at his house must have seen the Jeep in his driveway. So if they figure out that an SUV is missing from his garage? Well, I just don't want those who don't care for me to think that I stole it."

"He would verify it, though. Right?"

Was that a hint of doubt creeping into Derek's tone? "Of course. But he'd be at the hospital now with a gunshot wound. If he's in surgery or recovery, he wouldn't be able to answer right away." And if there were officers who didn't care for Reid, why would they bother asking Mr. Callahan when they could just harass Reid?

Samantha tossed him a perplexed glance as she drove under another streetlight.

Of course, Samantha.

"Derek, Samantha is here. She's his daughter, so we're good."

"Sure." But the hesitation in Derek's voice did nothing to calm Reid. "I'll see what we can find out after this latest incident, but as you know, these guys are good. We don't have much information on them."

"We have a little bit more now. Found what looks like evidence of embezzlement hidden on a flash drive. We got into that tight spot before I could email it to you, but it still doesn't help us as far as these guys' identities go. I'll get it to you as soon as I can." Reid tucked the phone back in his pocket. One more call was all he would allow, and then it was time for another phone.

He turned to Samantha, who was slumped in the driver's seat. "Why don't I take over? You'd probably like to rest after our getaway." Her skin glowed pink in the stoplight, her strawberry blond hair fairly aflame with the light shimmering around it. He could get used to her by his side. He cleared his throat and forced himself to look for a spot to pull over. "Here. Behind the strip mall. If those guys are paying attention, they might know what make and model we're in now, at least what they could see of it in the dark."

"I wouldn't mind getting out of the hot seat." She graced him with a weary grin, and his heart flip-flopped.

She pulled around the structure and turned in a circle until the SUV was pointed out again. As he climbed into the driver's seat, Lily roused in the back. "I want to sit next to Grandpa."

Samantha turned to look at Lily. "I think she's talking in her sleep. Her eyes are closed."

Reid pulled out and took a couple of rights until he had driven in a circle. What should they do now? They were all hungry, but it was late enough that everything in the sleepy suburb was closed. Should they try another hotel? In Thomas's SUV and with Reid's phone turned off, they should be safe.

Should be.

Perhaps another suburb altogether? But they had driven to a different area quite removed from Heartwood Hill, where Samantha's father lived, and the thugs had still found them.

He took a couple of lefts. No way did they want to sleep in the SUV again. Surely Derek would figure something out soon. The guy definitely had more resources than Reid.

But neither could he keep driving. He turned left again, only to see the same closed bookstore he had driven past a few minutes earlier.

Samantha roused from her drowsiness to look out the window. "Are we going in circles?"

"I thought you had your eyes closed."

"I can feel the motion of the car, too, you know."

Smart woman. It was just as much to her credit as it was to his that they were still out of the clutches of the bad guys.

"Can't we go to the hospital to check on my dad? Privacy laws are so strict that I don't think they'll tell me anything over the phone. I'd rather see him in person. Make sure he's okay. Look him in the eye and see if his change is genuine."

If only it were that easy…to see someone's truthfulness and intentions in their eyes. If it were, Samantha would have trusted him from the moment she rear-ended his Jeep. Her suggestion of the hospital was intriguing. It would be well lit, something in their favor since evil liked to conduct its deeds under cover of darkness. And the would-be kidnappers weren't after her dad, so they may not be monitoring him. But they might figure that Samantha would visit, though after the shooting, they ought to know that the cops would be all over the place.

"And what about food?" Samantha asked. "We never had our pizza, and I know Lily's got to be hungry. We could eat at the hospital."

"No. The hospital is too dangerous. I'm sorry, but they know you went to your father once." Five quiet minutes later, Reid pulled onto the interstate that led out of Heartwood Hill. "I have an idea, though."

From one difficulty right into something even more trying—that was what Samantha's weekend had been. She let her gaze follow the beam of the headlights, her fingers clutching at the fabric of her shirtsleeves, until she saw the sign pointing to the pull-off for the interstate rest area a few miles outside town.

"Now what? I don't want to sleep in the vehicle again."

"I don't, either." Reid swung the SUV in between two semis that had parked for the night. "But at this hour, there aren't many choices.

We can get a snack from the vending area and discuss our options. Like I said, I have an idea."

Reid was right, and Samantha blinked in the thick darkness in their secluded parking spot. "What about my dad? How do I get any information about how he's doing?"

"I'm not sure you can right now. But he's in the Lord's hands. Pray for him." Reid unfastened his seat belt and shifted in his seat. "I've seen a couple of wounds like his back in my days on the police force. The bullet will need to come out, so he's probably in surgery. Then it'll be a few hours in recovery and, eventually, physical therapy. Once this is all over, I'll drive you to the hospital myself."

Once this is all over. When would that be? She pressed a hand to her middle. Life had suddenly become tenuous...and precious. Was her father on a gurney, a standard-issue green hospital gown over his shoulders, a white blanket covering the rest of him? Were tubes and wires running every which way?

There was no way now that she could talk to him, look into his eyes, verify his change of heart and his recommitment to his daughter. His approval of her. All she wanted, all she had ever wanted, was to make him proud of her. Had they been close to that tonight?

Could people change? She swiped at the tears charting a course down her face. Reid seemed to think so. Maybe she ought to give Reid a chance, like she was willing to give her dad another chance.

As helpful and heroic as Reid had been, the danger was inching closer and closer with each run-in. Lily had suffered so much already, growing up without a mother and then the sudden death of her father, that Samantha ached with grief for the girl. Completely inexperienced at parenting, Samantha hardly knew what to do for her ten-year-old ward except to keep her fed and to provide a listening ear. Perhaps those were the most important things.

She fingered away her tears as Reid gestured toward the building at the rest area. "How about I get us something to eat? There ought to be a wide range of choices in the vending machines."

Lily perked up at the mention of food. "Sounds good to me."

Samantha leaned toward Reid to keep her question between them. "Are we okay here? Or do we need to watch for those guys again?"

"We'll always need to watch until they're caught. But I think we're okay here for a few moments. We're sheltered between these trucks."

He cupped her elbow, perhaps as assurance that he wouldn't be gone long. A pleasant warmth radiated up her arm and settled in her heart. It was becoming more and more comfortable to be with Reid, a fact that, ironically, made her more and more uncomfortable.

He lowered the windows a couple of inches, and a breeze ruffled her hair. "I'll scrounge up some snacks, hopefully something that doesn't taste too much like cardboard. Keep the doors locked, and I'll be right back."

As soon as the door closed, Lily scooted forward in her seat to lean against Samantha's shoulder. "I just met Grandpa tonight, and now he's at the hospital. Why did this happen to your dad?"

Samantha ached with renewed grief for the difficulties the girl had faced in her young life. Was Lily remembering the final moments she'd had with her own father? What could Samantha say to soothe her? "I don't know, sweetie. But he'll be all right. It'll just take some time. In the meantime, we need to pray for him. For his recovery."

"I prayed for my dad. He's dead now." Tears hovered in her eyes.

"I know, and I'm sorry."

"He got hit by that car, and they rushed him to the hospital, too. I saw him there, just like you just saw your father. But why did my father have to die? And yours gets to live?"

Anguish squeezed Samantha's heart like a vise. She wasn't God. She didn't know how to answer that. "My dad isn't just my dad. He's your grandfather now. He'll live and recover and be your grandpa."

Lily wrapped her arms around Samantha's middle as if holding on to a life preserver. "I guess so. But I still miss my dad."

"You'll miss him for a long time, although eventually it won't hurt as much. And you know that he loved you. Didn't he tell you that at the hospital?"

"Yeah. He said he loved me and that he was going to heaven where he would see my mom. And he called me by a nickname my mother made up. He never called me that after she died, until that night. So I know it was a big deal." Lily rubbed her face against Samantha's shirt as if drying tears.

"Your dad may not be here for you anymore, but God the Father is. He's always with us, guiding us and loving us and comforting us. As you grow up, I pray you'll learn to lean on Him more." *Your dad may not be here for you...* Samantha's own words reverberated around in her mind. For how many years had she pushed God and His guidance aside as she nursed her wounds from her father and from her college boyfriend? Apparently, she could dish out good advice but she couldn't follow it. The actions of her father and her ex-boyfriend had hurt her, but she had been letting that hurt dictate her attitudes for far too long. Just like she had told Lily, she needed to look only to the Father for comfort and love and acceptance. He would guide her to whatever was best for her.

Samantha turned to stroke Lily's hair away from her face. "The feelings we have after a relationship is over or when a relationship is difficult can hurt, but we can't let them control our lives. We have to keep going, trusting God to take care of us."

"What do you mean?"

"I mean relationships with fathers can be complicated, especially when we want their love and approval. Everyone is human and makes mistakes. But what really matters is the love and approval of God."

Reid returned to the SUV, his arms full of plastic tubs of sandwiches and bags of chips and bottles of juice. Samantha leaned across the driver's seat to open the door for him, and he stood still a moment, seeming to take in the two crying and smiling females. "Is everyone okay here?"

Samantha blotted a tear off her cheek. "You know, Lily, I'm sure even Mr. Palmer has had difficulties in his relationship with his father."

Panic streaked across his face as he sat heavily in the vehicle. "You could say that." A pain of some sort seemed to well up from someplace deep inside him, and he twisted in his seat as if he were sitting on tacks. He seemed to struggle to keep his tone level as he handed Lily a sandwich. "Eat something, and then we'll get going. Want to hear my idea?"

Samantha opened a bottle of tea and took a sip, waiting for Reid to answer further. But he wouldn't look away from the darkness outside the front windshield. Her eyes stung as more tears formed. There was some history there, a burden he carried with him, that affected his every choice and each interaction he had with others. But would he ever confide in her about it?

Did she even want him to?

FOURTEEN

Reid's idea for help was far more important than Samantha's little psychoanalysis session, but a glance at her told him she wasn't going to let it go easily. Sure, she had difficulty with her father. He'd cheated and left, both actions that destroyed families. Reid felt bad for her. But she had hope of reconciliation and time in the future to spend together. He had neither, unless he wanted to move into the state penitentiary and share a cell with the man he called Father. No, thank you.

His idea, though, could tie this whole discussion up in a neat little bow. He wouldn't bother talking about his biological father, the man who had passed the ever-destructive anger gene to him. He would focus on the father figure the Lord had sent to him all those years ago when the patterns passed on by his dad had finally caught up with him.

That father figure who could possibly save him…again.

Perhaps the expression on his face had warned Samantha not to pursue her line of questioning. Her next statement startled him in its bluntness, as if she had rebuilt that wall that had initially kept her distant and aloof. She wanted him to open up, to confide in her, but he wasn't willing. Probably never would be.

"I'm ready to go home."

Obviously, she thought she was in charge. But he hadn't given up his goal of making amends with his buddies on the police force and settling down in Heartwood Hill. He'd been through too much in the past couple of days to walk away now and let the entire community think he was a coward and a quitter. "You're not going anywhere without me. And we're not going to your home."

Samantha bristled like a threatened cat. "Look. My number one priority has not changed. Lily. Thank you for the snack, but we'll be fine."

"You absolutely cannot go home. Remember how those thugs tore your place up? They'll find you there. And if you don't like being under my protection, I guarantee you won't want to be in their custody." He wasn't ready to give up her presence, despite her bristles, but he didn't want to admit that even to himself.

"Fine. We'll sleep at my office."

"Where? In a plastic client chair? Does your desk chair lean back? Do you even have a sofa?"

Samantha glanced at Lily then back to Reid. A heartbeat later, a tear slid down her cheek, charting a course through her freckles that stood out against the paleness of her face. "I need normal, Reid. Lily needs normal."

He longed to brush away the dampness and touch the softness of her skin, but instead he shoved his hands into his pockets. "We all need normal. And we're going to have it back soon. This chase can't last forever. Someone will win, and I pray it's us. We have the police working on it, but I'm going to need your help, as well." He extracted a hand and touched her shoulder. "Now, why don't you and Lily use the facilities and dry your eyes, and then we'll get going. I need to make a phone call to secure our next move."

"Fine." Samantha and Lily scooted out of the car and headed to the restroom.

Reid had a clear visual line to the entrance. After the door closed, he shook his head. Statistics or not, he was still better off without the entanglement of a relationship. He'd explained the situation as best he could, doing his best to project empathy and feeling into his words just like he figured a woman would want, and all she could say was the innocuous *fine*?

"Whatever." His voice sounded loud in his ears with no one else there to hear his contribution to the scintillating conversation.

With the windows down, he had heard almost all of what Samantha and Lily had said. In fact, he hadn't really needed that long to purchase their snacks. He just didn't want to have to participate, perhaps because what Samantha had said to Lily had a bit of truth to it. A sliver of truth that pricked his conscience like a splinter.

He had suffered a lot of rejection because of his father and the genetic tendencies he had inherited. But did he really have to be like his father? What good was his salvation if it didn't truly and gloriously change him? Cross-examination had been a strength of his in law school, so now it was time to turn the tables on himself. Questions were the best weapon in an attorney's arsenal.

Reid removed the burner phone from his pocket and ran his fingers gently over the buttons. Could he truly change even though his father hadn't? Were the statistics right? Or did they not factor in glorious salvation and the help of the God of the universe? God was more powerful than any genetic tendency or string of statistics. Why couldn't he learn that once and for all?

He had the phone number memorized, and Bump had promised he was available anytime. But as Reid looked down to dial, his gaze caught on Lily's purple-hearts backpack resting in the backseat. He had no idea how she had managed to keep it close through all the running, but it had become like a third arm to the girl. Even in the commotion of escaping Samantha's father's house, she'd managed to drag it along. He snagged it from the bench and unzipped it. Perhaps there would be another clue inside that might lead them to whoever was jerking the strings of the thugs chasing them. They had found the flash drive, but was there more?

He pulled it open, disappointment slamming him in the chest at how little was in it. The torn-up memory book of her father was in there, which she had brought from their ransacked home. He flipped slowly through the pages, but there didn't seem to be any more information than what he already knew. It was simply filled with photos and memories of a happy life with Dad, as happy as it could be without Mom. Reid studied a photo of Lily's father, a recent one judging by Lily's appearance in it. He was not a standout guy, just medium height and medium build. But there was a spark in his eye that told Reid that he would not have stood down easily.

Reid laid the memory book on the front seat and pulled out a little stuffed panda bear. The fuzz on one ear was worn down to the nubs. The bear looked old enough to have been a baby plaything for Lily years ago.

There was also a coin purse with two quarters, a dime, three nickels and five pennies in it. Lily's life savings? It wasn't even enough to buy a fountain drink. He reached in again and removed her spy sunglasses. The only thing left was a worn copy of *Anne of Green Gables*. Reid hadn't read it, but he'd heard enough to know it was about an orphan taken in by an older couple. Reid's heart ached for the loneliness Lily must feel, his admiration for Samantha growing at her ardent desire to provide a home for the girl.

That was it, though. Reid scratched his chin. What about a secret compartment or something sewn into the lining? Maybe Lily was in possession of something desirable and didn't know it. He ran his hands over the outside and inside of the backpack, but he didn't feel any telltale bulge. Even a wad of money or a tiny flash drive would be noticeable under that scrutiny.

He returned everything to its place in the

backpack and leaned the bag back in the seat just as it had been. No sense upsetting the girl when her backpack hadn't provided any information.

Female voices sounded outside, signaling the return of Samantha and Lily. He checked his watch. It was after midnight, but his relationship with Bump was of the sort where time didn't matter, neither time apart nor the time of the call. He dialed the number just as Samantha slipped into her seat and swallowed a sip of tea.

Two rings later, a groggy voice answered at the other end of the line.

"Yeah, Bump? I need help."

The iced tea stuck in Samantha's throat, and she threw her hand up to block her sputtering.

Bump? Was that someone's name?

Lily shot her a quizzical look, but all Samantha could do was shrug her shoulders.

Reid met her gaze and nodded, as if that would answer all her questions. Into the phone, he said, "We're less than two hours away. Yeah, right away. Thanks. I owe you." He paused, listening. "Again."

Now what? Who was Bump, and what was his relationship to Reid? Reid had always seemed to be such a loner. She would never have pegged him as someone with a tried-and-true backup. She sipped her tea again, careful to let the coolness trickle down her throat.

Reid was like a two-thousand-piece jigsaw puzzle with over half the box missing. And she didn't really like puzzles. Who could he owe? And again?

He buckled up. "Let's get moving. It's time to try my idea of help."

The determined look on his face warned her not to ask any questions...yet. But she wouldn't spend too much time in that vehicle without knowing exactly where she and Lily were going.

Samantha buckled her seat belt and began her search. Her father had always kept stashes of just-in-case cash in lots of different places, and she had no reason to believe that his practice had changed, so it was just a matter of finding it in this particular vehicle of his. She pulled down the visor but only found the vanity mirror. Nothing was taped under the seat. But the pages of the owner's manual in the glove compartment revealed two hundred dollars in twenties. Wherever they were going, they had the money for the gas to get there.

Out of Heartwood Hill, Reid turned north on Interstate 65.

She gave him twenty minutes of solitude on

the highway before she began her interrogation. "So are you going to tell me where we're going and who this person is you call Bump?"

He started at the sound of her voice. "Bump is the man who introduced me to the gospel. He's the reason I'm not the same man you knew in law school. Him and Jesus Christ."

"Why do you call him Bump?"

"You remember back in the day, when those film-developing kiosks still sat in mall parking lots?"

It stretched the limits of her memory, but she could vaguely remember one. "Sure?"

"He attempted to bump one over. Armed robbery. He got caught, and while he was doing his time, he got saved. Gloriously, as they say. So now he pays it forward whenever he can, visiting guys who are stuck in lockup overnight waiting for charges to be filed or bail to be set."

"So he's a prison chaplain?"

"Unofficial. He ministers on the good graces of the officers."

Samantha stroked her neck but it didn't help her swallow over the lump forming. "How did you meet him?"

Reid cleared his throat and tossed a glance out his side window. "I was one of those guys."

Samantha failed to suppress her gasp. "So...
you were in prison?"

"Not prison. Lockup."

"It's still behind bars."

Reid pressed his lips together. The silence
stretched between them. She couldn't help
but stare at him, interrupted only by what she
hoped were furtive glances into the backseat
to check on Lily. When he refused to say anything further, she turned her stare to the shadows of stalks of corn rushing past her window.

Prison? She was riding in a car into the middle of nowhere with her ten-year-old responsibility in the backseat with a man who had
spent time in jail? What had he done to get
there? She fisted her hands on her thighs as
conviction settled on her like the weight of the
humidity that hung low over the cornfields.
Whatever had happened, it was over and done
now. He claimed to have changed, and as far
as she had seen so far, he had really and truly
changed. He'd been nothing but protective and
polite. Gentle, at times. Caring.

So why was it so hard to see him as anything
other than the rebel she'd known him to be?

In the end, it would be better not to take
the risk of knowing him or forming any type
of relationship with him, not even friendship.
She had her mother and her sister when they

came back from the conference, and she now had Lily. That was enough.

Reid drove about an hour and a half northeast on the interstate. He exited at a sign that was so faded it was barely legible. Only one gas station sat at the bottom of the ramp, and it was closed. Corn and soybean fields stretched for miles.

Reid pulled the SUV into the far corner of the gas station and cut the engine and the lights. Over Lily's gentle breathing, Samantha could hear legions of cicadas outside the window.

She peered into the darkness but didn't see a thing. "What are we doing?"

"Thought I saw a tail on the interstate. We'll just sit for a few minutes to make sure it's gone."

"If we're staying on the county roads, wouldn't the tall cornfields hide us?"

"Could, but they'd also hide a large SUV like we've seen those thugs drive."

He had a point. Samantha pinched her lips. Maybe it was better if she didn't ask any further questions.

Reid started the SUV again and pulled onto the narrow road, heading deep into farm country. Headlights flashed briefly behind them, then disappeared. Samantha turned to peer out the back window, but she couldn't see even a shadow in the little sliver of moonlight. Had they turned off their headlights? Just because she couldn't see them didn't mean they weren't there.

There was nowhere else to go. She prayed that this Bump would help them. Hide them.

The hour on the clock was in the single digits and the night was at its darkest hour when Reid pulled off the paved road and bounced the SUV down a gravel lane. The drive had made Samantha sleepy, and she fought to stay awake long enough to get herself and Lily into a bed.

An older man, about the age of her father but shorter and wiry, stepped out from the shadows as they approached a house and barn. He motioned them into the barn, jogging ahead to stop them at the proper place. As soon as Reid cut the motor and flicked off the headlights, the man closed the large door behind them.

Reid opened his door, turning long enough to Samantha to cock his head toward Lily and her door. Then he exited, and the older man she assumed to be Bump enveloped him in a warm embrace.

Samantha got out and opened Lily's door, reaching in to shake her awake. The child roused just enough to grab her backpack and stand, although she swayed on her feet like a newborn calf. Bump came around the front of the vehicle and wrapped them both in a tight hug. Up close, Samantha could see he had thick salt-and-pepper hair. A faint scent of aftershave mingled with the sweetness of hay. Samantha wanted to lie down right there and sleep through the rest of the night, but Bump whispered, "Into the house."

The trio followed him through a side entrance, through the darkness in between the buildings and into the darkened house. With much effort moving her feet to follow in her weary stupor, Samantha stumbled down a hallway and into a bedroom, or at least a room with a bed. With the door closed behind her, she kicked off her shoes and fell into bed. She was unsure of the surroundings, but Lily's slumbering form next to her soothed her into sleep.

Her next conscious act was to push her face into her pillow to block the bright morning sunshine streaming into the window and piercing her vision. A motorcycle revved outside, and she propped herself up on one elbow to look around. The room was simply furnished, its primary decoration dust at least a quarter inch thick. The quilt on the bed looked hand stitched, a lovely double-wedding-ring design in blues and greens. Apparently, at one point in Bump's life, there had been the touch of a woman. Samantha swiped her hair out of her face. Bump's story was probably one she would never hear.

She tucked the quilt around the still sleeping Lily and searched out the kitchen. It was time to meet Bump properly and see if he could make a good cup of coffee.

She found the kitchen at the end of the hallway, but not Bump. Reid sat at the white enamel table, sipping from a steaming mug and reading a newspaper. His presence summoned images of domestic tranquility, and Samantha blinked a few times to get her concentration back on the tasks at hand: coffee and getting her life back.

With one step into the kitchen, Reid looked up and smiled. "Coffee's in the pot. Cups are in the cabinet just above."

"Thanks." She reached into the white metal cabinet and retrieved a cup, then poured and held it to her nose, allowing the rich aroma to push her eyes open a little farther.

"Sleep well?"

"Yes, although I was so tired I don't think it would have mattered if I had slept sitting up on a hard bench." She pulled out the chair across from him and sat gingerly, setting her mug on the table. "I was thinking about Lily's great-aunt Beatrice."

"Great-aunt? You think she might be behind this attempted kidnapping?"

"I doubt it, but she's the only person I could come up with who would have any interest in Lily."

"Why? What's the relationship?"

"She's Lily's father's mother's sister." She sipped her coffee. "Lily's father's aunt. She thinks that Lily ought to be in her charge because blood is thicker than water."

Reid snorted into his cup. "What gives you that idea? If she's a great-aunt, she's probably physically incapable of caring for the girl."

Samantha stiffened at his poke. "Actually, that's what she said to me. Those words. So I just wondered if it might be her behind all this, trying to get control of Lily since she's the closest blood relative."

"You know all this from the guardianship proceedings?"

Samantha nodded. "I know it seems like a crazy idea. Beatrice's health is failing, and she's in no shape to care for a child. Plus, she never really knew Lily so she has no relationship with her. She lives on the other side of the country. Washington State. If Lily went to live with her, she would never see the people she knows and is growing up with from church and school. It's not in Lily's best interests."

"Is it realistic, though, that this great-aunt would hire these thugs just to kidnap her great-niece? Why wouldn't she just dispute the guardianship petition?"

"She did. That's how I know of her presence and desires. But Lily's father had enough foresight to change his will in the year before he died to appoint me guardian." She sipped her coffee. "I'd thought of calling Beatrice, just to see if I can determine what's going on. See if she's crazy enough to hire those guys to kidnap Lily."

Reid waved his hand as if to dismiss the conversation and stood, crossing to put his mug in the sink. "Don't bother. How could it be her? I just can't see a little old lady engineering all we've been through. Some people just want to make a stink, but when push comes to shove, they back off."

"Then, we could eliminate her as a possibility."

"Look, if it isn't her, there's no sense in alerting her to danger. If it is her, then our call could alert her to our location." He gestured toward the laptop on the breakfast bar. "Besides, I've looked a little more thoroughly at the flash drive. I can't tell who's moving money, but it wasn't a great-aunt from the other side of the country." He turned back in the doorway. "I'm going to find Bump. Catch him up, get a ride and some ammo. Extra towels are in the bathroom across from your room if you and Lily want to shower." With a goodbye tap on the doorjamb, he was gone.

Samantha sat back in her chair, holding her cup to her lips. The prior warmth and welcome of the kitchen disappeared with Reid, and she clanked her cup back to the table. So much for the daydream of domestic bliss and the longing for a normal family life.

FIFTEEN

Reid stepped out into the late-morning sunshine, a sneeze tickling him as he squinted at the glare off the motorcycle that rested on its stand near the barn. Samantha, her hair tousled from sleep, her face fresh and innocent in the morning light, had been a welcome sight, an instant brightness in Bump's shabby kitchen. He could definitely get used to seeing her beautiful face every morning.

Except for when her expression had turned to dismay. Had he been harsh with her? Too quick to dismiss her ideas about this great-aunt Beatrice? But what was he supposed to say? In his experience, little old ladies rarely warranted suspicion of that sort. Beatrice had made her presence known to the new girl in charge of her niece, and now she had laid claim to birthday cards and Christmas gifts and occasional visits. Her position of authority in the family had been established. That was all she wanted, Reid was sure of it.

He rubbed his neck as he sauntered past the motorcycle and toward the same barn door they had exited in the middle of the night. Reid was sure Bump would be in there by this time of day, caring for his collection of bikes and muscle cars like some men cared for horses.

Bump was an amazing man, and Reid agreed with him on every subject except one.

Motorcycles.

If there was one thing Reid would never do again, ever, it was to get on a motorcycle.

He stepped inside the barn and latched the door behind him, standing still to let his eyes adjust to the dim interior. The barn had been revamped and cleaned with a cement foundation poured. Still, the pitched roof and the scent of hay lingered. Bump was several yards away with his back to the door, rubbing down the hood of a classic GTO. "Your coffee hasn't gotten any better, Bump." Reid raised his hand in greeting as his old friend turned. "Same blend, same pot."

"And I guess you remember where everything is." Bump leaned against the hood as Reid approached. "How you doing?"

"Could be better, but I'm grateful for your

help. Trying to make a normal life for myself, and I end up right back here."

Bump nodded, the weight of understanding bowing his head. "What about the woman and her daughter?"

"Samantha's up. Lily will be soon."

"I'm sure you know, but you probably shouldn't stay here long. You can get some sleep, get some hot food. But it sounds as though those guys are on a mission and aren't going to rest until they've accomplished it."

"I figured."

"When you go, you can take a ride. Just not one of my babies." Bump grinned and winked at Reid.

"I wouldn't dream of it. And I'm not taking a bike." Reid crossed his arms in emphasis.

"Now, listen. I know you had that little difficulty with a motorcycle. Well, a few different cycles. But that was a long time ago. And you're a changed man now. I know. I saw it. I nurtured it right in there." He nodded toward the door that led to the house then met Reid's gaze with a steely look. "And in here. You'll be fine."

It sounded like such a sure thing when Bump said it. Reid knew his faith had changed him, so why didn't he feel different all the time? He let his gaze wander over the several cycles

Bump kept. A tremor crept through him at the image of climbing onto one again.

He grabbed a chamois and worked by Bump's side, and a comfortable silence settled between them. It felt good to be in the company of a man who encouraged him in his walk with the Lord, and a peace he hadn't felt in a long time alighted on his spirit.

The sun had changed position, shifting the beams of light that filtered through the high windows, by the time Samantha and Lily appeared in the doorway.

They had both showered, and Samantha's reddish hair looked as if it had just been tousled by a towel. Apparently, she had enough confidence to appear without a bunch of feminine primping and fussing. She was adorable.

Reid stepped toward her, unable to stop the grin that crawled across his face. "Feel better?"

She nodded as Bump appeared next to him. She stuck out her hand to shake his. "I'm so sorry for intruding on you, but thank you for letting us crash so late last night. I'm Samantha Callahan. This is Lily." She nodded toward the girl.

Bump smiled at Lily then turned his attention to Samantha. "Don't think anything about it. I'll do whatever I can to help Reid and anyone he vouches for." He turned toward Reid and slipped him a wink. "And if he's told you what he should have about me, you already know I'm Bump."

Reid jammed his hands into his jean pockets. A teenage feeling of awkwardness swept over him, and he stared at the floor, wondering what Samantha's expression was.

"Did you find something to eat?" Bump said.

Lily jumped forward and wrapped her thin arms around Bump's right arm. "We saw the eggs and bacon still on the stovetop and the two plates in the sink, so we figured the rest was for us. Was that all right, Mr. Bump? It was delicious."

Bump laughed and laid his free hand on her shoulder in a half hug. "That's why they were there. We're not formal here. Take what you need. And just call me Bump. No Mister."

"Why are you called Bump?" She let go of his arm but continued to stare up at his cragged features.

Bump glanced at Reid. Reid shook his head slightly. The girl didn't need that sort of introduction to the world of criminal behavior just yet. If she hadn't heard when Reid had told Samantha earlier, then she didn't need to hear now.

"We'll talk about that some other time, munchkin." Reid ruffled her hair.

Bump tugged her toward the door and tossed a nod at Reid. "Munchkin? Can I call you that, too? I have a mother cat with some kittens just a few weeks old living around my back steps. Why don't you take Reid and see if they'll come out?"

"Yeah!" Lily bounded out of Bump's grasp and grabbed Reid's hand. "Come on, Mr. Palmer."

Reid let himself be tugged toward the door. Apparently, Bump wanted to talk to Samantha alone. That could only mean one thing.

As he stepped into the afternoon sunshine, Reid prayed that Bump would have the discretion not to say too much.

Samantha ran her hand through her hair, fluffing it out to dry. She had no idea why Bump wanted to talk to her without Reid present, but she prayed that she could hear it with grace. Her emotions had been stretched like a rubber band over the past few days. One more pull, and she might break.

Bump watched out the door, presumably to see Reid follow Lily to the kittens, then pushed it until it was ajar and turned to Samantha. "I know we just met, so please forgive me if you think I'm butting in where I don't belong."

She nodded, the only response she could muster until she'd heard him out.

"I've known Reid for a few years, and I've come to know him quite well. So I can tell how he feels about you. I can hear it in his voice and see it in the way he looks at you."

"Really?" That was not what she'd expected to hear. At all. And yet, her traitorous heart beat double-time, revealing what she had already suspected, even hoped for, if she were to admit it.

"But he's scared, and here's why." He paused and glanced toward the door. "He thinks he can't be trusted with a wife."

"What? Because of his anger?" Wow. Her admiration for Reid bumped up a notch.

"It's a little more than that. He's read all the studies and discovered that sons of abusers are much more likely to become abusers. He doesn't want to risk that with a woman who might become his wife, so he's decided he's better off without one."

"His father beat him?"

"Not him. His mother. But you can imagine the anger that stirred in him and his brother. They were just little boys and had to watch their own dad lash out in anger."

"Where are his parents now?"

"His dad's in the state penitentiary. His mom's in the cemetery."

Samantha clutched at her chest, her breathing quickly turning shallow. It was hard to imagine what a terrible childhood Reid must have suffered. "So that's why?"

"Yeah. He became a police officer because he wanted to battle wrong. He thought it was the best way to combat the evil he had seen as a child. But he still didn't have that anger under control. So when he was chasing someone on a motorcycle trying to elude arrest, he got angry. Next thing he knew, he had his police motorcycle up to nearly one hundred forty miles an hour."

"One hundred forty? I didn't know motorcycles could go that fast."

Bump nodded. "Yep. Obviously, that's against procedure. One incident like that can be overlooked. But two more times? No way. And when he lashed out against the bike, kicking it and tearing it apart in his anger, that was it. His superior officer came down hard on him. He wasn't fired exactly, but it was strongly suggested that he leave the force."

"That's when he went to law school."

"You remember what happened there?"

"I've been puzzling over it these past few

days. He always seemed angry, so much so that most of the students didn't like to be around him. Toward the end of the first year, he got upset with a professor in class and yelled at him, calling him names. Very disrespectful."

"Again, it was suggested that he move on. So he transferred to another school. He hadn't resolved his anger problem, and he got into an altercation when he accused a fellow student of plagiarizing his work. Reid hit him and ended up in the lockup waiting for a charge of assault and battery."

"That's where you met him." Puzzle pieces were coming together, and Samantha's heart melted for Reid's struggles.

"He told you."

"Only that much."

"I spent half the night with him and left him with a Bible. He was desperate to hear the word of God and the hope and help it would bring him. I've not often seen a young man so eager and so quickly changed. He apologized profusely to the other student and no charges were filed, but it was too late to finish a degree at that school. He found one last law school and finished his degree there without further mishap, after I talked with the dean and gave him my assurance that Reid would be fine."

"Where's he been the past couple of years?"

"Working here and there. But he feels as if Heartwood Hill is his home, and he wants to reconcile with his former brothers on the police force. He left with some hard feelings, and he wants to make it right again."

Samantha sputtered, a cough caught in her throat. "I messed that up for him. When I ran into him, I made him take me to the police station. He wasn't ready to go, and it didn't work out well." She fluttered a hand to her neck. But what about his desire to practice family law in Heartwood Hill? He would be a direct competitor to her practice. Could the town support that many lawyers?

Her feelings for him were real, though, no matter how much she tried to deny them. Did love always work out, like all the songs suggested? Or would their job situation get in the way? What happened next? Her heart seemed to melt inside her, puddling with understanding and sympathy for a man who had worked hard and embraced faith to change from a life of wrong to a life of right. A man who was a gentleman and a warrior. A man who had put his very life on the line to rescue her and Lily.

Bump ahemed loudly, drawing her back to the barn and the vehicles and the fact that they were on the run from kidnappers. Love would have to wait. Perhaps forever. "One sure way to tell he's not the same Reid is his aversion to motorcycles. It's almost as if he thinks that if he rides again he'll revert to that old controlling anger. I've told him that's not true because he's living in the power of Jesus Christ to change lives, but it's a tough go for him."

Reid's voice filtered in through the door, getting louder as he got closer, telling Lily he needed to talk to Bump. Bump leaned into Samantha and whispered, "Keep praying," then moved away before Reid stepped inside.

"I appreciate your hospitality, Bump, but we need to get a plan together." Reid's baritone struck a chord in Samantha's spirit, and she found herself staring at the floor, heat crawling up her neck. "We have the flash drive filled with evidence of embezzlement, but you don't have internet way out here in the boonies, so I can't email it. I thought we'd call my buddy Derek and meet up with him. Deliver the goods in person."

"Of course." Bump held up his hands in surrender as he approached the door. "You two plot your course, and I'll go help Lily coax those kittens out. She'll do better with a bowl of milk, and I wouldn't mind spending more time with that charming young lady." He winked, and in a moment, he was gone.

Alone at last. Samantha shook her head.

Why did that pop into her mind? She might understand Reid better now, but that didn't mean she was ready for a relationship. Men were completely off her radar and had been for years. There was no reason in the world why that should change now.

Was there?

The faint sweet scent of hay wafted to her nostrils, and she rubbed her nose with the tickle. Light filtered in through the high windows in the converted barn, and for the first moment since the entire awful ordeal had begun at the church, she felt a measure of peace.

Reid broke the silence with a crack in his voice. "Once a cop, always a cop, the saying goes. I just can't sit back and wait for Derek and the others to find our perps, especially when we have crucial information." He scratched his hands on his jeans, then grabbed a chamois and began to rub it over the closest motorcycle in tight circles.

"That's why I wondered about Lily's greataunt. I guess you picked up on what I was trying to say before about that conversation." She meandered toward the bike and ran her fingers over the closest handlebar.

"Do you have any other ideas? An acquaintance of Lily's father? Could it be someone disgruntled with your representation?"

"Adoption is, for the most part, a happy practice. Who would be disgruntled?"

Reid crossed his arms and leaned against the bike. Quiet contemplation hung thick between them.

Samantha summoned a mental image of her client list, running through names and faces, but no one stood out. No one had been unhappy with her representation. And she had no idea who Lily's father's business acquaintances were.

A creaking sounded from the motorcycle as it began to tip precariously toward her legs. It fell against her, the seat pushing on her hip. She stared at it, frozen, as all she could do was picture being pinned under the large machine. In a fraction of a moment, before she could react and escape the crush of the bike, Reid dashed around to her side and grabbed the bike. He leaned into it, forcing it back upright.

Samantha covered her mouth with a shaking hand and sagged against Reid's straining biceps. She had been rescued again by the man she had doubted. He secured the bike, one arm wound around her waist to hold her upright, as well.

"I know it's been a fast couple of days, but

I need to say something." The warmth of his voice wound around her heart and drew her closer. "We've actually known each other several years, and before we're on the run again, I want you to know." He swallowed, his Adam's apple bobbing in agreement. "I think I'm falling in love with you."

Before she could respond, he reached to pull her hand away from her mouth. Her breath caught in her throat with his closeness, her heart pounding in rhythm with his as safety and security and strength enveloped her just like his arms. He lowered his lips toward hers, pausing as an invisible connection of their spirits surged between them. His gaze flicked up to look in her eyes, then back to her mouth as he gently touched his lips to hers. All her doubts were thrown to the wind. This was right. He was falling for her, and now she knew she felt the same.

The bang of the door startled Samantha away from the warmth of Reid's embrace.

"Eww!" Lily stood in the doorway with a kitten in her arms.

Reid stepped backward, pulling Samantha's sense of sanctuary with him, and seized that opportunity to move back to the other side of the motorcycle. He quickly knelt down and fiddled with the kickstand, a flush coloring his face.

Lily shot a quizzical stare at her, a sloppy grin splayed across her lips. "Can I have a kitten?"

SIXTEEN

What a moron he was.

Reid grabbed the cloth again and jerked it across the motorcycle. What a moment, wonderful and horrible at the same time. Wonderful because he could get used to that closeness to Samantha. Horrible because he shouldn't. What had he done?

He'd told the truth. He was falling in love with her. What that meant from here, he had no idea. But at least she knew, and they could figure it out later.

Samantha let out a sigh. Reid dared to glance at her, but he couldn't read her expression. "No, Lily. No kitten. Maybe another time, when everything settles down."

Lily's shoulders sagged, and she disappeared back outside.

Samantha turned to Reid, her blue eyes ablaze. Was it love that shone in her eyes? Did he dare to hope? Or was it rejection? He had to stop her before she could say she didn't feel anything for him. Before his mortification was complete. "I'm sorry." His voice was husky with remorse. "That was completely inappropriate. I must not be thinking straight with this heat. Please forgive me."

She waved her hand as if to dismiss his apology. "We have to figure this…this problem… out. There's no reason why Lily can't have a kitten, except for the one, giant, horrible fact that we're on the run from guys who want to kidnap us. The girl should have a regular childhood filled with play and books and a cute, cuddly pet. Are we ever going to be back to normal again?"

Reid spun to grab the closest tool within reach, an air-pressure gauge, and checked the motorcycle's tires. Normal? What exactly was normal anyway? Perhaps Samantha had achieved it, but he didn't even know what it looked like, felt like, tasted like. Could his new normal possibly include the red-haired beauty who was worrying just a few feet away? He ached to embrace her again, run his hand through her waves, whisper to her that he would take care of her and all would be well.

Instead, he tossed the gauge onto the worktable with a clank. If he ever found normal, it wouldn't involve a wife. Maybe he would get a dog. Man's best friend.

Reid meandered to the doorway and leaned against the frame, rubbing his arm against it. "You'll have normal again. Derek's working on it. I'm working on it. Now Bump is working on it. We'll figure this out." *Eventually*, but he didn't say that out loud.

Lily sat near the porch to the house, facing the barn, a bowl of milk next to her. She had stretched out her hand and was calling for the kitties. Reid watched her, admiring her tenaciousness. At some point, she had retrieved her spy sunglasses from her backpack and worn them outside. Smart girl. The summer sunshine blinded Reid, and he arched his hand over his eyes to shield them.

She must have noticed his movement, for she glanced up and waved at him just as Samantha joined him in the doorway.

His throat thickened, an ache rising in it. Would he have a family someday? A family like they must appear—loving father and mother in the doorway watching their daughter romp with the kittens? He swallowed down the lump. He could never have his heart's desire. At least, he shouldn't try to have it, not with his family history.

The mewing of a kitten drew Reid's attention. Lily sat stiff, seeming to stare straight ahead. She had forgotten about the kittens cavorting around her knees. "Mr. Palmer? I see something flashing in my mirror. You know that little mirror inside my spy glasses? Is it light glinting off something? Sunlight?" She turned and pointed down the lane. "See? Is there a car coming?"

Samantha backed away, her hands fluttering to clutch each other at her chest. Reid stepped farther out and stared down the lane, raising both hands to shield his eyes from the sun. The afternoon sunlight slanted down the dirt road, and he squinted hard as the sweet and sour smell of the surrounding cornfields filled his breaths.

There it was. A flash of sunlight reflected on something. He strained to hear the hum of a motor. A moment later, a rumble vibrated in his ear.

"Lily, leave the cats." The girl ran to him, and he squeezed her shoulder as a comforting gesture. "Thank you for that alert." He called into the barn after Samantha. "We need to go."

Samantha appeared in the doorway, her eyes wide, her arms hugging her middle.

"I'm armed and so is Bump, but I don't want to get into a firefight if we can outrun them. We need to deliver the flash drive anyway, so let's get moving." His voice carried across the yard, and soon Bump came running out of the house, Lily's backpack in hand. "You expecting anyone, Bump?"

Bump nodded down the lane. "I saw from the kitchen window and grabbed my binoculars. That's no one I know." He led them into the garage and grabbed a set of keys from a rack on the wall. "Take the Mustang. That's your only hope to outrun them. And you'll be safer enclosed in a vehicle."

Without a word, only fright engraved across her face, Samantha hugged Lily close and looked at the car, waiting for Reid to make the first move.

Reid followed close to Bump toward a highland-green Mustang Bullitt. He leaned close to keep his voice low. "That's a classic. I can't take that. Think what it's worth."

Bump turned and put both hands on Reid's shoulders. "Think what you're worth. Think what Samantha and Lily are worth." He pulled Reid toward the vehicle and thrust the keys at him. "You're taking it. You'll be fine."

Reid's legs felt like lead. He glanced over his shoulder at Samantha pushing Lily into the middle of the front seat, Bump holding the door. This time, though, there was more at stake. And it wasn't his frustration or anger or lack of control driving him. It was the need to protect the woman—the two women—he loved.

But what if? What if he couldn't outrun them? What if his anger returned? What if he proved to himself and to Samantha that he wasn't truly a new man?

With a hand on his back, Bump pushed him toward the car. "Go!" As Samantha and Lily secured themselves with shaking hands, Bump hit a button to open a garage door at the back of the renovated barn. "Come on! You don't have much time! It's your only hope for outrunning those guys. You know that." Bump stepped up next to him and laid a strong hand on his forearm. "I'll say it again. You'll be fine."

Reid's legs disobeyed his mind, and he found himself swinging down into the seat. He started the machine and inched toward the door, a movement of air through the open windows ruffling his hair and his spirit. His only hope was to outmaneuver them.

Samantha grasped Lily's hand in her own perspiring palm, her body pressed up against Lily's in the front seat. Dizziness threatened to engulf her as her mind spun in an effort to completely understand where she was and what she was about to endure.

After everything that Bump had told her about Reid, this was their escape? But there wasn't time to analyze. Reid had his hands wrapped around the steering wheel and was gently leading the Mustang toward the back of the barn and the open door that would lead them straight into trouble. Lily trembled beside her, grasping her backpack.

She tore her gaze away from the woods outside long enough to steal a glance at Reid. There was a grim set to his mouth. Was he upset that they were on the run again? Or was it a comfortable determination?

"You'll be fine," Bump hollered over the roar of the engine.

Reid nodded as Bump backed away and turned to a storage locker. Was he going to retrieve a weapon to cover for them in their escape? He couldn't possibly outgun them. Not just one man. Was he grabbing a helmet to ride along with them? But then Reid revved the car, and the rush of the wind through the open windows whipped away all further wonderings.

Lily squeezed her hand. The poor girl had tears in her eyes.

Samantha leaned toward Lily and squeezed her hand back. "We'll be fine," Samantha shouted to her, repeating Bump's mantra. She prayed it would prove to be true. Lily nodded and sucked in her lower lip to try to stop the tears.

Why couldn't they just figure this out and make it stop? Why not give the thugs what they want, the flash drive or whatever it was? Money. Information. Anything to make it all go away.

"Lord God," she prayed aloud. "Protect us. Save us. Be with Reid as he steers us." A prayer spoken in desperation was just as effective, if not more so, as one carefully designed and transcribed. Never before had one of her prayers been so fervent, so heartfelt, so needy as those few words.

"Amen!" Reid and Lily hollered at her side.

Lush green cornfields flew by at a dizzying rate. Dust rose up and blew in through the windows, tickling her nose and choking her throat. The crops soon morphed to woods, and she leaned toward Lily in the middle, an instinctive avoidance as tree branches scraped across the Mustang. She closed her eyes to stop the motion sickness that threatened upheaval in her stomach. When a leaf slapped her in the face, she popped her eyes open. If the chase, and her life, were going to end in a collision with a tree, she wanted to see it coming.

SEVENTEEN

Where was the road? Reid would wipe the sweat from his face and neck if he dared to take a hand off the wheel. For now, other matters were more pressing than his personal comfort. Like his life and the lives of his passengers.

He needed to get them to a road, anything away from the woods, where the limbs and leaves were flapping into the car—plus, this well-worn dirt path didn't allow for much speed. Samantha cowered down in the seat, Lily huddled against her. Reid drove, his attention back to the path ahead just as a deer leaped in front of the vehicle. He slammed on the brakes and narrowly missed the white tail of the animal, but the roar of the monster SUV following filled the forest.

Several yards ahead, a shimmer drew his attention, the mirage of wavy lines as heat met a length of asphalt. Pavement, at last. Safety and speed were within his reach.

Maybe.

And if he did save Samantha and Lily, if they were able to escape and catch the bad guys and resolve the whole ordeal, what did that mean for him anyway?

The bump onto the asphalt pushed a grunt out of him. As the tire treads caught traction on the pavement, he leaned into the steering wheel, urging it to carry them to safety. The Mustang handled well. Still, though, he couldn't seem to elude their pursuers.

The car's odometer inched toward three digits as greens and browns and blues rushed by at a bewildering pace. The SUV revved a couple of yards back.

A bullet pinged just outside the window, puffing up the dust and leaves at the side of the road. A second bullet struck the side mirror and ricocheted into the field.

"Keep your head down!"

Samantha and Lily instantly ducked, tucking their heads as far down as they could manage in the tight space.

They didn't want him. They only wanted him to stop so they could get Samantha and Lily. As long as he was able-bodied, he wasn't going to voluntarily stop the vehicle. They would have to shoot more than the dirt.

Another shot buzzed past his window, a narrow miss as he blasted around a curve.

He floored it on the straightaway, but another bullet pinged next to him. He focused on the road ahead. It would take more than that.

The steering wheel jerked in his hands as a flapping sounded from the back of the Mustang. A bullet had hit one of the back tires. What had worked for Reid before would work for the thugs now, and Reid strained against the wheel to keep the vehicle from careening off the road.

The second rear tire popped, and he cried out with the sudden exertion of controlling the car. He sensed, more than saw, Samantha's surprised turn of the head.

Perspiration popped out on his forehead as he struggled against the wheel. If he slowed, they would be captured. But if he couldn't control the vehicle, at that insane speed, not one of them would survive a crash.

The sting of defeat spasmed in his chest, and he released his foot from the gas. The car immediately slowed, but Reid couldn't risk a crash with his impaired ability to steer safely. Most likely, this wouldn't end well, and he had failed Samantha and Lily. Not only would he not get the girl, but he would never be able to practice law in Heartwood Hill. He would forever be known as the lawyer who hadn't been able to protect that poor Samantha Callahan.

How could he go on without Samantha anyway? There was no other like her.

As he continued to slow, the steering wheel jerked out of his hands. He hit the brakes as the Mustang careened off the road and into a thick mulberry bush.

Disappointment engulfed Reid like the cloud of exhaust that came from behind. Even more upsetting than the end of his career was the knowledge that he wouldn't have a chance at a relationship with Samantha. Despite his history and family background, he wanted to put his best efforts into a relationship with her. There was something about her that compelled him to be the best he could be and to continue to keep his past in the past, with her at his side and with God's help. But now, even if they survived this, she wouldn't want a protector who couldn't protect.

With the car stopped, he turned to Samantha and Lily. They met his gaze with wide eyes, but both seemed unhurt. He shot up a prayer for guidance and help as the two thugs approached, malicious and victorious smiles smeared across their faces.

Samantha tugged on his arm and pulled him close. With tears in her eyes, she swiped a kiss across his cheek. "Thank you," she whispered. "My defender. My hero."

Reid just shrugged his shoulders, but his heart felt as if it would burst from the pounding of love through his arteries. She didn't seem disappointed in him at all. Scared, perhaps. Terrified, even. Not many had traveled at that speed. His determination to get through whatever was coming doubled.

"Out of the car," one growled. The other approached the passenger side and motioned Samantha and Lily out. Both had their weapons trained at the Mustang's passengers.

Samantha and Lily clambered out as Reid exited the driver's side.

"Now hand it over."

Reid reached down to his ankle holster and handed his gun to the thug.

As Reid's captor marched him around the car to join the females, Lily shot out her foot and kicked the thug closest to her in the shin. The big man dropped with a groan, surprised by the sudden move and the accompanying pain. As the girl dashed toward the cornfield, Samantha ground her heel into the top of his foot.

The man nearest Reid pointed his weapon toward Lily.

"No!" the injured man hollered at his companion. "He says he wants her alive." He hobbled toward the spot in the tall corn where Lily had disappeared. "I'll get her. You manage these two."

Samantha's lips began moving fervently, and Reid joined her in prayer for Lily's safe escape. Prayer that she would be able to get back to the safety of Bump's place. Prayer that the girl would know which way to run. Perspiration dotted her brow, but he couldn't tell if it was from the intensity of her prayer or the chase.

The remaining thug holstered his weapon, then pulled some rope from a pocket in his cargo pants and tied their wrists loosely in the front. When he had finished, he removed his weapon again and swung it around on his finger. As so often happened with arrogance, the man's cockiness made him dangerous, and Reid stepped in front of Samantha to protect her should the gun go off.

A few minutes of waiting by the side of the deserted road with no vehicle approaching in either direction convinced Reid that there was almost no chance anyone would come along who could and would help them. If they were to escape from this, it would be up to him and Samantha.

A moment later, a nondescript white cargo

van pulled up. The thug guarding them opened the back and pushed them inside, then stepped up himself. At the wheel sat a small pale man. Without a word, he slammed on the gas and the tires squealed in his eagerness to get to a new destination.

For nearly an hour, Reid gazed at Samantha's blue-eyed, strawberry blonde beauty, trying to communicate love and encouragement through their eye contact. He didn't dare to speak. For one thing, as a captive, he didn't want to risk angering his captors. For another, he didn't want to give them any more information than they already had. Samantha gazed back, her lip trembling intermittently, the little lines around her eyes crinkled with worry.

Eventually, the van stopped, and they disembarked outside a small, windowless brick building that stood several yards from a two-story office building. "I know that building," Samantha murmured as she seemed to stumble closer to him. "Lily's father worked there."

"No talking," the pale man ordered.

The thug pushed them inside, and Reid, even in his relative technological ignorance, recognized it as some kind of communication center with servers and cables and wires set out in careful arrangements. The man sat in front of a laptop at a plastic folding table as the armed roughneck slammed the door shut behind them.

He grasped a wireless mouse and turned to Samantha with a slight grin. "I suppose you're wondering why I've called you here today." He snorted through his nose. "I've always wanted to say that. Sounds lawyerly."

Samantha shot Reid a look. The guy was nuts. Reid inclined his head toward the man to indicate to Samantha that she should humor him.

"You and the girl are hard to catch up with, especially with the help of your boyfriend. I thought putting a hold on your bank account would stop you, but now I think I'll just keep your life savings as payment for my trouble. See, I need something that you possess, and I'll have my guys do whatever is necessary to get it." The thug stepped toward Samantha, and she shrunk where she stood.

Reid struggled to put the pieces together. The guy who had showed up just as they were captured. The office building where Lily's father had worked. The way the man with the sunless skin commanded the big guys with guns. The information on the flash drive. He cleared his throat to get the little guy's attention. "You're him? The guy behind all this? You're all in this together?"

The man at the computer shook his head, but Reid couldn't tell if he was surprised at the audacity of speaking up or just curious at how Reid had come to his conclusion. "Seriously? Look at me. I hired these guys. They'll do the job, I'll pay them, then they'll disappear without saying a word to anyone. That's what they do for a living."

"Do what job?"

The man nodded to the thug, who approached Reid and began patting him down. With one pat on his pants pocket, the thug reached in and retrieved the key chain. "That it?"

"Bring it here." The man sneered. "Awful pretty key chain for a manly man like you." He grabbed it and examined it for a moment, then stuck a dirty fingernail in the middle of the heart and pried it apart. A grin snaked across his face. "Let's get this plugged in. If it's what I been looking for, then I might let you go. Then I'm going to escape to a country without an extradition treaty, so I don't need to plead the Fifth. Isn't that what you lawyers say?" He jerked the mouse in little rectangles. "I used to work with the girl's father at the pharmaceutical company. But that nine to five was getting a little tiresome, and the retirement money wasn't adding up like I wanted. So I helped myself to a whole lot of retirement money. Problem is, someone found out and copied my files before I could move the money. The girl's father. He always was a do-gooder. He was on his way to deliver the evidence to the police, but I stopped that. Yeah, I saw the flash drive. But he'd passed it to the girl before I could get it."

"You embezzled and hid the money."

"Look at me. I know I'm nothing to look at. Short. Receding hairline. Never married and always rejected. For decades I've toiled at that company. Given them far more than the requisite forty hours a week. I'm sick of it. I'm escaping this boring life and going to live on the beach somewhere, where I'll be lauded and revered because I'll be a rich American."

"Why chase Lily, though? And Samantha? You have the flash drive now. Let us go." Reid wiggled his wrists in an attempt to loosen the ropes. If he got loose, he had no idea what he'd do, but he'd take his obstacles one at a time.

"Nah, I don't think so. I've put a lot of time and effort into this, finding the picture of the girl and her guardian, searching them down, locating the tracking information the girl's father put on the flash drive. I watched the girl for a while and saw her relationship with the woman, and I figured I better grab the guardian, as well. I didn't figure on you, and you made this much more difficult than it needed to be."

A growl issued from Samantha as she twisted her hands against the binding. This man had better watch out if the mama bear got loose.

If Reid kept the guy talking, would the man lose his focus, making an escape possible? Reid had learned in his police training that worked in domestic disputes to calm down attackers, but this was a far cry from that type of situation. He racked his mind to think of what to ask next when the only door banged open.

Lily stood in the doorway. The second thug slouched behind her, pushing a gun into her back.

"Lily!"

Her beloved Lily stood in the doorway, but Samantha couldn't embrace her. She struggled against the rope but couldn't loosen it from her wrists. Samantha had always believed in the wonderfulness of adoption, but to experience it herself? As mother, not as lawyer? Well, nobody had better hurt her girl, for a love that was deep and fierce burned in her soul for the child of her heart.

"Are you okay?" Her voice scratched against her throat. "Did they hurt you?"

The first thug towered over her. "Zip it, lady."

As best she could from this distance, Samantha scanned Lily from head to toe but didn't see any injuries. When Lily stepped into the building, she seemed to be walking normally. No limping.

Lily caught her gaze and nodded slightly. Samantha prayed that was an acknowledgment that Lily might be winded and sore and sticky from the corn slapping against her as she'd run, but that she was unhurt. Samantha expelled a force of air that made her hair tickle against her face and doubled her resolve to give her life, if need be, to protect Lily. Judging by the look on Reid's face, he had determined the same thing.

The man with the gun pushed Lily toward Samantha and then returned to his post outside, leaving one thug and the mastermind at the computer in the tiny building with Reid, Samantha and Lily. The man at the laptop nodded at Samantha. "You know now why you're here. Let's see if this is what I need."

Lily rushed toward Samantha and wrapped her arms around her middle. Samantha ached to be able to hold the precious child, but right now she needed to stay strong. Later, when it was over, if it was ever over, they could cry and hug and never leave each other's sight. Reid shuffled where he stood, drawing her attention, and she met his steely gaze. Yet lurking behind his slate-blue eyes was a love and compassion that overflowed for the both of them.

"All right, all right." The bad guy pulled Lily away from Samantha.

Samantha swallowed. She would try to be as gentle as she could. The poor girl had been through so much she didn't need more evil shoved at her. "Sweetie, this man wanted that silver heart key chain that your father gave you before he died. Remember that key chain?"

Lily chewed her bottom lip and darted glances around the room. She was obviously distracted by their surroundings, but who could blame her?

"It's here," he growled. "This is it." He turned to Reid. "Now, who else has a copy? Did you make a copy or email these spreadsheets to anyone? The police?" With barely a pause to let Reid answer, he pressed him again. "I haven't got all night. Your time's running out."

Reid growled back, "Listen, buddy. You ever hear of duress? Forcing someone to act contrary to their interests, especially when they are falsely imprisoned, doesn't exactly aid in remembering. Chill out."

The man stood, nearly an entire foot shorter than Reid, and held his gun to Reid's abdomen. "You know what? You're expendable."

"No!" Samantha heard the screech before she realized it was her own voice. "Just give us a minute." She turned to Lily, who now had large tears welling in her eyes, and forced herself to gentle her tone. What could she say to the girl to distract her from the anguish unfolding before her? "Look at me. It'll be fine. Think back to those final moments with your father in the hospital. He died because he prevented this man from stealing a lot of money from the company. Your father was doing a wonderful thing, so let's remember him as a hero."

Lily hiccupped as tears rolled down her face. "We didn't have very long because he was hurt so bad—"

"I know, I know. Shh. It's all right." Samantha shot a pleading look to Reid, then returned her focus to Lily. "I remember that you told me your father said some tender words to you. You had a few special moments with him right before he died."

Lily nodded.

Samantha leaned down but didn't risk stepping closer to Lily. "Didn't he call you by the nickname your mother used to use? The nickname your father hadn't spoken since your mother passed away several years ago?"

Lily was silent, swiping at the tears that cascaded freely.

The thug approached and nudged Samantha in the ribs with his gun. She flinched at the contact. "Enough of the blubbering. Dry it up."

"Hey!" She turned a stern look on him. "Have some compassion." Her heart leaped into her throat at her own brazenness, and she swung her gaze to see what their captor's response would be.

He barely widened his eyes and nodded at the thug. The man stepped back, and Samantha let her attention slide by Reid. She inhaled deeply to steady herself, although it didn't work as well as she had hoped.

Reid's eyes widened, and a slight grin like the Cheshire cat's crept across his lips. Did he like her spunk? Considering his past as a rogue police officer, probably so. And of course, a kiss didn't lie. She shook her head to clear thoughts of Reid. She needed to focus on the task at hand—saving Lily and herself.

The man slapped the table, and Samantha startled. He stood and sneered at her. "Come on. It's been a touching little reunion, but I still need an answer. Did you make any copies?" He enunciated as if he were addressing a kindergartener.

Samantha looked to Reid and nodded.

"No," Reid said.

He turned back to the computer, the thug with the gun peering at the screen, as well. Another weapon rested on the folding table.

Samantha shook some stray hair from her face. Now that the bad guys had the flash drive and all the information they apparently wanted, would she and Reid and Lily be killed? There was no point in keeping them alive, especially since he had told them his plans. It was probably just a matter of minutes before he turned his gun on them. Lily knew Samantha loved her, but did Reid? She had never told him and now she wouldn't have the chance. Ever.

With their attention focused on the monitor, Reid tapped his shoe on the floor to get Lily's attention. Samantha jerked to attention. Was now the moment for final, silent goodbyes? But as she watched, he twisted his wrists against the rope to dig his phone out of his front pocket and pass it to Lily. The lure of success had apparently made the villains lose their vigilance in guarding their captives.

A satisfied smirk crossed the man's face. He stared at the screen intently and rubbed his hands together. "Ha! I'm in, and soon, all will be secure."

With all attention fixated on the computer, Reid nodded to Samantha. He knew what he was doing. She would trust him. Peace settled on her as she realized that she did trust him. Implicitly.

With one last glance and sly smile, Reid stamped his foot on the floor and coughed. The man at the computer didn't move, but the thug spun toward the sound. As he faced Lily fully, she flashed the camera light from Reid's phone in his eyes. With the man temporarily blinded, Reid bounced his knee into the man's abdomen. As the thug doubled over in pain and fell to the floor, the small man swiveled from the computer. Before he could retrieve his hired thug's gun, Reid stepped in front to cut him off. The small man landed his fist into Reid's gut, but the blow was weak. As Reid pushed him against the wall with his chest, his wrists still tied, the door burst open. Several police officers with weapons drawn advanced into the tiny space. Reid's buddy Derek was at the head.

In a matter of moments, the weapon was confiscated, and the man and his thugs were handcuffed. Samantha and Lily were loosed, and Samantha feared her heart would explode as she gathered Lily in her embrace.

Derek clapped Reid on the shoulder and removed the rope that bound him. Reid rubbed his wrists as he approached Samantha, a question arching his eyebrows. She curled a finger for him to join their happy hug. His warmth enveloped her, the sense of safety and security making her knees weak. Without his arm around her and Lily, she would have fallen to the floor.

As the villain and his hired men were led out, Bump stepped in. Reid broke away from the little group, and Samantha led Lily but refused to remove her arm from around the girl's shoulders.

Bump shook Reid's hand and pulled him into a manly hug. "Everyone okay?"

"Now we are. Do we owe thanks to you?"

Bump shrugged. "After you took off from my place and those two crazies zipped by on their cycles, I followed. I was too far behind to help you. But eventually I saw the Mustang crashed into the bush. Obviously, something was wrong, so I called the police. It was touch-and-go in a few places, but we were able to follow the van's tire tracks."

"Thanks." Reid pulled Bump in for another hug as Samantha felt mist fill her eyes. Few things were as attractive in a man as his affection for a father figure and the desire for a relationship of iron sharpening iron. "How many times over now do I owe you my life?"

"No one's counting."

Derek called for Reid from his position at the computer. "We got here at just the right time. Between the laptop and the flash drive, everything is here, and the account is still open. That'll save our guys a ton of trouble, and all the money can be returned to the proper owners."

Samantha rubbed her hand across Lily's back and planted a kiss on her forehead. She thanked God for a safe conclusion to the mad chase of the past couple of days. In the end, it had all come down to the love of money. She shook her head in wonder and praised God for her satisfying law practice, for her family, for Lily and for Reid. She and Lily would never have survived if not for his protection, of that she was sure.

Reid tugged on her hand, his smooth, cool palm pressing against hers, and walked her toward the door. A smile lit his face, a happiness illuminating him that Samantha could get used to seeing every day. "Can I give you a ride home?"

She stepped outside, pulling him behind. He

opened his arms to her, and she moved into his embrace. Darkness enveloped them, but she felt as if she could light up the night sky with her joy that the events of the past few days were over. Better yet, she had found love and acceptance and security with Reid. She nestled her head against his strong shoulder. "I love you," she whispered.

Reid tightened his arms around her and kissed the top of her head. "I love you, too."

EPILOGUE

Two months later

Crackling leaves swirled around Samantha's ankles as she stepped from Reid's Jeep. She tugged her jacket closer to ward off the autumn chill in the air as Bump approached from the house.

"Howdy!" Bump's relief at the end to their trial shone in his smile. "How was the drive?"

"Gorgeous." Reid came around the vehicle and slid an arm around Samantha, his gaze never leaving her face.

Samantha slipped away and hugged Bump. "The fall colors are perfect. Thanks for having us."

"It's my pleasure." Bump looked at Lily. "The kittens have grown and lost some of their shyness. And I got a couple of pumpkins to paint, and I've loaded up the wagon with hay for a hayride. What do you think?"

Lily nodded eagerly and turned to Samantha. "Can I go see the kittens, Mom?"

Samantha's heart warmed at the title that was now becoming familiar to both of them. "Sure. We'll catch up."

Bump and Lily took off, and Reid grasped Samantha's hand to saunter toward the barn. "It's been quite a couple of months, hasn't it?"

"Definitely. With the adoption finalized, Lily's now calling me Mom, although I think we're still getting used to it. It doesn't roll off her tongue yet, but it will in time."

"Last time we saw your dad, I noticed she seemed comfortable calling him Grandpa."

"Isn't it amazing how that relationship is being restored? I never thought I'd look forward to spending time with Dad, but now that he's found faith, it's wonderful. He and Mom are talking again, too." Samantha crunched on some leaves, the autumnal sound a welcome relief after the heat and humidity of the summer.

"As long as we're talking about how life has improved, what about your upcoming trip to Gatlinburg?"

"Lily is so excited about that, she pulled out her suitcase last night even though it's not for another week." After the finalization, a celebratory trip seemed to be in order. Their first vacation as legal mother and daughter. And now that the bank had released the hold on Samantha's accounts and all was straightened out after the man who they'd found out was named Boyd Deel had had his fun with her, she had the funds for a little travel.

Yes, after that little detour, life was now headed in the right direction. Samantha couldn't think how it could get any better.

With Bump at the wheel, a tractor pulling a wagon of hay sputtered to a stop in front of them. "All aboard!" Bump called.

Lily sat on the hay directly behind Bump and pursed her lips. "We're not a train," she teased. She slipped on her spy sunglasses in the late-afternoon sunshine.

Reid helped Samantha onto the back of the wagon, then sat next to her. With a glance back to verify everyone was secure, Bump threw the wagon into gear. It jerked ahead, and Samantha leaned into Reid to try to stay upright. His grin told her he didn't mind being her support.

With the setting sun filtering through the canopy of crimson-and-pumpkin-colored leaves, Reid leaned close to Samantha. "I was thinking that after you and Lily get back from your weekend trip, perhaps we should start planning a honeymoon. Just you and me for a week."

Samantha couldn't stop the smile that started in her heart and spread across her face. She tipped her head with what she hoped was a quizzical look. "Is there something you want to ask me?"

Reid brushed her hand against his lips. "Samantha, will you marry me?"

Samantha's heart pounded. Perhaps life could get just a little bit better. "Gladly."

He leaned toward her to seal the engagement with a kiss. As his soft lips touched hers, her life was complete.

"Eww," Lily cried from the front. She reluctantly pulled away from Reid to see Lily turn and pull off her spy sunglasses. Lily and Bump smiled at them like a couple of jack-o'-lanterns, and Reid squeezed Samantha's hand.

"Like I said. Just you and me."

* * * * *

Dear Reader,

Thank you for reading my debut novel!

I was worried about Reid and Samantha, their safety and their chance for love. Weren't you? They have both been through so much in their lives that it was easy for each to think that he or she not only wasn't capable of a successful relationship, but didn't deserve one. Reid was a new man as a result of his new faith, but he continued to doubt that the old man wouldn't come back. His protection of Samantha finally convinced him that his faith was real and that God wouldn't abandon him. Samantha grew to embrace her coming legal motherhood and was determined to provide a normal life for her charge. They both learned that God gives second chances, not only in their love for each other but in His love for them. His mercies are new every morning!

I would be honored to hear from you. You can visit my website at www.meghancarver.com or email me at meghanccarver@gmail.com.

Many blessings to you,
Meghan Carver

LARGER-PRINT BOOKS!

GET 2 FREE LARGER-PRINT NOVELS PLUS 2 FREE MYSTERY GIFTS

Love Inspired®

Larger-print novels are now available...

YES! Please send me 2 FREE LARGER-PRINT Love Inspired® novels and my 2 FREE mystery gifts (gifts are worth about $10). After receiving them, if I don't wish to receive any more books, I can return the shipping statement marked "cancel." If I don't cancel, I will receive 6 brand-new novels every month and be billed just $5.49 per book in the U.S. or $5.99 per book in Canada. That's a savings of at least 19% off the cover price. It's quite a bargain! Shipping and handling is just 50¢ per book in the U.S. and 75¢ per book in Canada.* I understand that accepting the 2 free books and gifts places me under no obligation to buy anything. I can always return a shipment and cancel at any time. Even if I never buy another book, the two free books and gifts are mine to keep forever.

122/322 IDN GH6D

Name _____ (PLEASE PRINT)

Address _____ Apt. #

City _____ State/Prov. _____ Zip/Postal Code

Signature (if under 18, a parent or guardian must sign)

Mail to the Reader Service:
IN U.S.A.: P.O. Box 1867, Buffalo, NY 14240-1867
IN CANADA: P.O. Box 609, Fort Erie, Ontario L2A 5X3

Are you a current subscriber to Love Inspired® books and want to receive the larger-print edition?
Call 1-800-873-8635 or visit www.ReaderService.com.

* Terms and prices subject to change without notice. Prices do not include applicable taxes. Sales tax applicable in N.Y. Canadian residents will be charged applicable taxes. Offer not valid in Quebec. This offer is limited to one order per household. Not valid to current subscribers to Love Inspired Larger-Print books. All orders subject to credit approval. Credit or debit balances in a customer's account(s) may be offset by any other outstanding balance owed by or to the customer. Please allow 4 to 6 weeks for delivery. Offer available while quantities last.

Your Privacy—The Reader Service is committed to protecting your privacy. Our Privacy Policy is available online at www.ReaderService.com or upon request from the Reader Service.

We make a portion of our mailing list available to reputable third parties that offer products we believe may interest you. If you prefer that we not exchange your name with third parties, or if you wish to clarify or modify your communication preferences, please visit us at www.ReaderService.com/consumerschoice or write to us at Reader Service Preference Service, P.O. Box 9062, Buffalo, NY 14240-9062. Include your complete name and address.

LILP15

REQUEST YOUR FREE BOOKS!
2 FREE WHOLESOME ROMANCE NOVELS IN LARGER PRINT
PLUS 2 FREE MYSTERY GIFTS

·

HEARTWARMING™

·

Wholesome, tender romances

YES! Please send me 2 FREE Harlequin® Heartwarming Larger-Print novels and my 2 FREE mystery gifts (gifts worth about $10). After receiving them, if I don't wish to receive any more books, I can return the shipping statement marked "cancel." If I don't cancel, I will receive 4 brand-new larger-print novels every month and be billed just $5.24 per book in the U.S. or $5.99 per book in Canada. That's a savings of at least 19% off the cover price. It's quite a bargain! Shipping and handling is just 50¢ per book in the U.S. and 75¢ per book in Canada.* I understand that accepting the 2 free books and gifts places me under no obligation to buy anything. I can always return a shipment and cancel at any time. Even if I never buy another book, the two free books and gifts are mine to keep forever.

161/361 IDN GHX2

Name _____ (PLEASE PRINT)

Address _____ Apt. #

City _____ State/Prov. _____ Zip/Postal Code

Signature (if under 18, a parent or guardian must sign) _____

Mail to the **Reader Service**:
IN U.S.A.: P.O. Box 1867, Buffalo, NY 14240-1867
IN CANADA: P.O. Box 609, Fort Erie, Ontario L2A 5X3

* Terms and prices subject to change without notice. Prices do not include applicable taxes. Sales tax applicable in N.Y. Canadian residents will be charged applicable taxes. Offer not valid in Quebec. This offer is limited to one order per household. Not valid for current subscribers to Harlequin Heartwarming larger-print books. All orders subject to credit approval. Credit or debit balances in a customer's account(s) may be offset by any other outstanding balance owed by or to the customer. Please allow 4 to 6 weeks for delivery. Offer available while quantities last.

Your Privacy—The Reader Service is committed to protecting your privacy. Our Privacy Policy is available online at www.ReaderService.com or upon request from the Reader Service.

We make a portion of our mailing list available to reputable third parties that offer products we believe may interest you. If you prefer that we not exchange your name with third parties, or if you wish to clarify or modify your communication preferences, please visit us at www.ReaderService.com/consumerschoice or write to us at Reader Service Preference Service, P.O. Box 9062, Buffalo, NY 14240-9062. Include your complete name and address.

HW15

YES! Please send me **The Montana Mavericks Collection** in Larger Print. This collection begins with 3 FREE books and 2 FREE gifts (gifts valued at approx. $20.00 retail) in the first shipment, along with the other first 4 books from the collection! If I do not cancel, I will receive 8 monthly shipments until I have the entire 51-book Montana Mavericks collection. I will receive 2 or 3 FREE books in each shipment and I will pay just $4.99 US/ $5.89 CDN for each of the other four books in each shipment, plus $2.99 for shipping and handling per shipment.*If I decide to keep the entire collection, I'll have paid for only 32 books, because 19 books are FREE! I understand that accepting the 3 free books and gifts places me under no obligation to buy anything. I can always return a shipment and cancel at any time. My free books and gifts are mine to keep no matter what I decide.

263 HCN 2404   463 HCN 2404

Name	(PLEASE PRINT)	
Address		Apt. #
City	State/Prov.	Zip/Postal Code

Signature (if under 18, a parent or guardian must sign)

Mail to the **Reader Service:**
IN U.S.A.: P.O. Box 1867, Buffalo, NY 14240-1867
IN CANADA: P.O. Box 609, Fort Erie, Ontario L2A 5X3

* Terms and prices subject to change without notice. Prices do not include applicable taxes. Sales tax applicable in N.Y. Canadian residents will be charged applicable taxes. This offer is limited to one order per household. All orders subject to approval. Credit or debit balances in a customer's account(s) may be offset by any other outstanding balance owed by or to the customer. Please allow 4 to 6 weeks for delivery. Offer available while quantities last. Offer not available to Quebec residents.

Your Privacy—The Reader Service is committed to protecting your privacy. Our Privacy Policy is available online at www.ReaderService.com or upon request from the Reader Service.

We make a portion of our mailing list available to reputable third parties that offer products we believe may interest you. If you prefer that we not exchange your name with third parties, or if you wish to clarify or modify your communication preferences, please visit us at www.ReaderService.com/consumerschoice or write to us at Reader Service Preference Service, P.O. Box 9062, Buffalo, NY 14269. Include your complete name and address.

MMLPBPA15

READERSERVICE.COM

Manage your account online!

- Review your order history
- Manage your payments
- Update your address

> *We've designed the*
> *Reader Service website*
> *just for you.*

Enjoy all the features!

- Discover new series available to you, and read excerpts from any series.
- Respond to mailings and special monthly offers.
- Connect with favorite authors at the blog.
- Browse the Bonus Bucks catalog and online-only exculsives.
- Share your feedback.

Visit us at:
ReaderService.com

RSI!